Moonpool Revelation

By

Kingsley Taylor

Grosvenor House
Publishing Limited

All rights reserved
Copyright © Kingsley Taylor, 2023

The right of Kingsley Taylor to be identified as the author of this
work has been asserted in accordance with Section 78
of the Copyright, Designs and Patents Act 1988

The book cover is copyright to Kingsley Taylor

This book is published by
Grosvenor House Publishing Ltd
Link House
140 The Broadway, Tolworth, Surrey, KT6 7HT.
www.grosvenorhousepublishing.co.uk

This book is sold subject to the conditions that it shall not, by way of
trade or otherwise, be lent, resold, hired out or otherwise circulated
without the author's or publisher's prior consent in any form of
binding or cover other than that in which it is published and
without a similar condition including this condition being
imposed on the subsequent purchaser.

This book is a work of fiction. Any resemblance to
people or events, past or present, is purely coincidental.

A CIP record for this book
is available from the British Library

ISBN 978-1-80381-730-9

Dedication

To Joanne, who Moonpool calls Little Rainbow's daughter, who has sprite blood in her.

To Jonathan
   & Esther

Simply Biden

[signature]

Preface

Some years ago I took an MA in Celtic Christianity at Lampeter College, for my dissertation I did the history of the Group of parishes I am Vicar of from the end of the Roman Occupation to the beginning of the Middle Ages. While researching this I found so much archaeological evidence of earlier times, so I continued doing research back to the end of the last ice age, 10,000 years ago. I wanted to write a novel based on the development of people from the earliest settlers, but how to do this? I discovered St Mary's Church is built in an elliptical enclosure (or a henge) in line with the rising of the asun of the equinox. Early one equinox morning I watched the sun rise to check the alignment, the penny dropped, I met Moonpool and this then is the continuation of her story from the end of the first book.

Contents

Chapter 1	Empty Throne	1
Chapter 2	New Way	5
Chapter 3	Winter Solstice	11
Chapter 4	Marcus Quasitor	16
Chapter 5	Roman Occupation	24
Chapter 6	Hard Decisions	30
Chapter 7	The Underground	37
Chapter 8	Battle Prevented	42
Chapter 9	The Missionary	50
Chapter 10	Eochaid Allmuir	56
Chapter 11	Castell Dwyrain	62
Chapter 12	Rival Brothers	66
Chapter 13	Saint Canna	71
Chapter 14	The Exorcism	81
Chapter 15	Hunting Party	89
Chapter 16	White House	95

Chapter 17	Hermit Sten	102
Chapter 18	Abbot Pierre	107
Chapter 19	Steady Growth	113
Chapter 20	New House	118
Chapter 21	Brother Andrew	123
Chapter 22	The Dreamer	129
Chapter 23	Great Pestilence	138
Chapter 24	Ladies Circle	146
Chapter 25	The Rebellion	153
Chapter 26	Restored Faith	157
Chapter 27	The Investigation	162
Chapter 28	Silent Watcher	173
Chapter 29	Local Trouble	182
Chapter 30	Cyffig School	189
Chapter 31	Iron Road	195
Chapter 32	Seeking Fairies	203
Chapter 33	Three Sisters	208
Chapter 34	New Vicar	211
Chapter 35	Moonpool Revelation	216

Chapter 1

Empty Throne

I have waited a few times before but not like this. I have waited with a human while on Earth, but not before with my own kind. We all waited. And I mean all. I stood with Arberth, behind and above us the sprites of streams and trees and flowers, Gronw and Marlais were there and an empty place where Little Rainbow should have been. Below us were the greater spirits including Arianrhos and Lleu Llew Gyfhoes, below them were the messengers that now using a Greek word were referred to by humanity as angels, the many ranks of angels with the Seraphim around the throne silent. The beings whose place it was to worship The Maker Of All Things constantly throughout time were silent, they also waited.

They were silent because the Throne was empty.

The Son of The Maker Of All Things was dead and The Maker Of All Things was gone.

If any of us actually breathed we would all be holding our breath.

We waited for existence itself to end.

None of us were at our posts, we were all here. How the universe didn't implode without us I suppose The Spirit Of The Maker Of All Things could maintain it all quite well without us, we were never really needed anyway, but how was he active when he, The Maker and the Son were One anyway, I did not understand.

Yet here we were, gathered round the empty Throne.

The Son had died to save humanity. Because The Maker Of All Things is not bound by time this very act saved all the human souls who had died stretching back throughout history, but would there be more to come? Would there be a future?

The Earth rolled on without us, the whole universe spun and danced without us, but the rolling of the earth, my main concern, rolled oh so slowly and for someone for whom time is still an enigma this was as much as I could bear. But with the Throne empty why should I be concerned at the slow rolling of the earth, I was empty inside I could have no meaning myself.

My valley turned towards the sun and I was not there. The people of the valley went about their lives unaware.

We all stood silent, unmoving, the five and five and five and five and four elders sat still on their thrones with their crowns on their laps, the seraphim stood silent for the first time in their existence. There were no rumblings of thunder, no flashes of lightning, the sea before the Throne was dark. All of us had the same thought, could this be the end of all existence?

The Earth rolled on and took my valley into the night.

Any gathering of humans is never silent, they fidget and cough, rub imaginary itches, for they cannot keep still. But we were, not a sound, not a movement.

Had the whole of creation come to this? The humans had a special place in the plan of The Maker Of All Things and despite all that they did his Son went into the world and was one of them. The utter arrogance of humanity to think they could kill him, and yet kill him they did.

All creation should end. All creation ought to end. But what of The Maker Of All Things?

The universe continued to dance and spin. The humans went about their lives as if nothing had happened except a few frightened people in the land where he had lived his human life. My valley rolled slowly on back into the light of the sun.

We were all still here, though we waited, and what for? Three days he had said, three days, then what?

I tried to remember some of the things I had heard, I tried to reason, but I could not. Beyond being aware of the empty Throne, the gathering of all spirits, the absolute silence and the continued spinning of the universe I was too numb to think.

And my valley rolled back into the night.

Then everything changed. All was light and joy, The Maker Of All Things was on his Throne and his Son with him. None of us could look, the Son bore his scars and we could not bear the sight. We all fell prostrate before him.

Exactly what happened next I do not understand.

"Moonpool." Came the voice.

"Son Of The Maker Of All Things." I answered still prostrate.

"Moonpool, stand."

I couldn't yet I could not disobey so somehow I stood but kept my head bowed.

"Return to your valley. I go to my people and they will spread the message, the war is won but there is still so much to do. Your role will change but you will still be needed from time to time."

I had questions but in His presence you have no questions. So I simply returned.

I sat on the bank where Ban's bones were and gazed about me.

Owain, now an old man, was standing at the altar and stopped in the middle of lighting the fire in one of the pots from a burning brand. His mouth was open as if in the middle of reciting something.

I could not understand how I was in physical form, Owain did not have sufficient belief and no one else was around. I must ask Arianrhod when I meet with her.

"P....p....p " Owain tried to speak.

"Owain, your niece Aderyn, has she returned from Clunderwen yet?"

Stunned silence.

"When she does return send her here."

Owain slowly walked backwards bowing constantly until he was outside the enclosure. I sat for a while longer while I still could. Only now as I reflected on recent events did it strike me how many spaces there had been round the Throne. How many of us had become human? How many had simply been forgotten and fallen asleep? I would not now become human but how long before I was completely forgotten and fall asleep? I drew comfort from what the Son had said, that I would still be needed from time to time.

Chapter 2

New Way

A few days later the Moon was full and Aderyn returned from Clunderwen with the oak staff. She stood in the holy place gazing up at the Moon nervous and excited. It was a still night, there were no clouds in the sky to hide the stars, no breeze ruffled the leaves, the river gurgled in its course, the bats flew back and forth and an owl hooted in the dark.

How I was able to appear before I do not know and Arianrhod knew no more than I did, except that all spirits had been told the same thing by the Son in the twinkling of an eye as if they were the only one. Perhaps it was by His authority? But now it was Aderyn's belief in me that was strong enough for me to appear in physical form so I stood with her and I listened to the night sounds, I breathed in the cool night air.

"Moonpool." She used my old name and humbly got down onto her knees.

"Aderyn." I lay my hand on her shoulder. "Do not kneel to me for I am a creature as you are."

"But you are a goddess."

"Aderyn, do not kneel to me, I am not a goddess. I may be spirit but I am still a creature made by

The Maker Of All Things. I am a servant." And I smiled my winning smile.

Slowly she stood. There was confusion on her face.

"Just because you don't understand something you should not fear or be in awe or feel yourself any less. You humans have a special place in The Maker's plans."

She thought for a while. "And you?"

"I do not know. I simply do his bidding."

"Something has changed." She looked around her for a moment. "I felt it a few days ago."

"Yes, but it is not up to me to tell you it is a matter for human kind, news will come soon enough." I knew a man named Joseph was already leaving his home country and was on his way to this island, a place he had often traded with.

"Why did you want to see me then?" She gazed back up at the Moon and only glanced at me briefly.

She was tall and rather heavily built, she wore the now traditional robes of a druidess of simple woven cloth dyed earth brown and dull green, her russet hair tied in a braid that reached down her back to her waist and her eyes were a pale and searching blue.

"I have had no human contact for such a long time, I have missed that. Whatever I am supposed to do I am granted that."

She turned and smiled. I felt she was the one searching my innermost being with her penetrating, intelligent eyes rather than the other way round.

"We were told your kind had left, we were told this was the age of humanity and you were no longer needed. I'm glad that isn't true. When you asked to see me I thought we could not drive your kind away, after all, you are more powerful."

"It is partly true. This is not my time, it is the age of humanity and I am not sure what my part in this is, I was hoping we could work this out together."

"I don't understand. You have been here so I believe from the time of the first settlers, you have watched over them and protected them, so you must know everything."

"I know many things but I do not know everything and the more I learn the more I realise I do not know." I smiled wistfully.

For a while neither of us spoke. I gazed up at the Moon, so bright and cold and distant, in many ways Arianrhos was my mother except I was never born. Yet even she did not understand where we were now or what our place was.

"Another thing." Aderyn glanced at me again. "I thought you would be taller."

"Taller? I am the whole valley, I am that ridge where the old stone druid's hut is," I waved my arm to the south, "I am way up the Marlais to the fort beyond Vel Dref," indicating the west, "I go way up the Gronw to the fort where they keep the cattle." indicating the north.

"And the east?" She asked after a pause.

The memory of Little Rainbow still troubled me. "I don't go far that way."

"Your request to see me sounded urgent. Why did you really want to see me?"

"Much has changed. I am older than you know and I have seen the slow formation of the Earth, the coming and going of the ice. But since I have become involved with humans I have seen change happen time and time again in what I would consider a short period. I usually know nothing of the future but a small amount of knowledge has been given me that I am compelled to pass on to you. The changes that are coming will be swift even as you would consider swiftness. The first change will be gentle, do not resist it, I can say no more because it not my place to say. The next will be brutal and dangerous. I don't know if it will come in your lifetime but I fear your people may be swept away, try and reason with the newcomers if you are to remain, try to make peace so you are not swept away."

"You will protect us."

"I am the valley and I am nature, I have no authority over the wills of humans. I will do what I can nonetheless for I do have powers you cannot know."

The Sun rose and set many times, rose to its fullest, sank to its least and rose to its fullest again four times. Then a man came from the south, an island fort of the oak trees. He was dressed simply as a druid in a coarse woollen robe tied at the waist with a flax cord. He had an oak staff with the name Yeh-shu-ah in Hebrew lettering carved on it. He followed the wooden road and took the simple track into Sarnlas, entering the village he paused for a moment to catch his breath.

There were quite a few people around at the time and they all stopped to see what this visitor wanted.

"Good people, I have travelled far to bring wonderful news that will change your lives." His face almost shone with joy.

Aderyn had been tending an old woman near to death but sensed something was happening outside the hut as everyone had fallen silent apart from the one raised voice she did not recognise and she caught the word 'change'. She emerged and saw the stranger.

"You must be the holy woman of the village." He addressed Aderyn seeing her simple dress which was typical of female druids.

"I am Aderyn and I have been expecting you." She greeted him.

"And I am Branok. I bring good news." He paused a moment. "You were expecting me?"

"Yes. I will explain later, but you said you have wonderful news."

"News of joy and hope, news of eternal life."

"Then perhaps you can help, come, meet Ffion and if indeed you have wonderful news you can give her hope before she dies."

Somewhat taken aback Branok followed her back into the hut, many of the villagers gathered round the entrance to hear.

Pausing for a moment to let his eyes adjust to the dim light within then he looked down with compassion on the old and feeble Ffion, her face thin and drawn. Branok knelt down by the dying woman and took her hand.

"Ffion, do not be afraid. The one you know as The Maker Of All Things has come to Earth in person of his Son, he has lived a human life, has died to end death and returned to life again that we all may live. This is a mystery yet we know that The Maker Of All Things has compassion for all people."

She looked up into his eyes and saw the faith and sincerity there. She looked across at Aderyn. Aderyn crouched down beside her and looked questioningly at

Branok who nodded reassuringly then smiling Ffion took her hand.

"Is this true? Can it be?" Ffion asked in a weak voice.

"I believe this is what Moonpool was hinting at so it is true, though this is a lot to take in." She looked from Ffion to Branok, now was not the time to ask him the questions that burned within her.

"Ffion." Branok smoothed her brow. "He waits for you with open arms, do not fear."

Her breath came easier although it was very shallow. She looked back at Branok and smiled a weak smile. No one moved for some time. I felt a familiar presence and she slipped quietly away into his keeping. Her last sigh was a sign to the humans that she had died and Branok closed her eyes.

There was silence for a while then Branok looked across at Aderyn. "Do you understand?"

"It is a lot to take in, I am not sure I understand."

"You said you were expecting me and you spoke of someone called Moonpool. Has someone been here already with the good news? I know many of us have been sent out but I don't know a Moonpool."

"I was told someone was coming and I should accept the change he brought, I can say no more. I want to hear all your news and I am sure the people here will too."

Later as they gathered round in the space between the houses to share food Aderyn asked Branok to explain to her and the villagers what he meant about the Son. So late into the night he told them the news, his face alight with gladness. But it is not my place to tell these things.

Chapter 3

Winter Solstice

Aderyn and her brother Idwal, Cheiftain of the valley, stood outside their round house in the early morning and the newly risen sun low in the sky shone on the mist in the valley. Many seasons had come and gone since the visit of Branok and very little had changed except Branok had Spent a day instructing Aderyn, baptised her in the river and laid his hands on her in blessing to commission her in the service of the Son before he left. From then she had incorporated the new teaching into her rituals and blessings. They looked back along the road towards the East where it dipped beyond the hills. The sun was already bright in the sky and although the weather was fair there was something dark and brooding in their thoughts.

"We know what Moonpool meant by the gentle change." Aderyn said at last. "And we have accepted that and I know the truth in my heart. But what of the brutal change?"

"Could she mean the Romans? They invaded the South East before, they may come again and this time they may invade the whole land. If they come here our whole way of life will change."

"Rome has been defeated before."

"I know but mostly by peoples more violent than them. I don't know which would be worse."

"If it hadn't been for Moonpool's warning I would have said we are too far away from all those peoples."

"At least we will get some warning. However, the attack could come from Erin, they have attacked before and they are a wild people."

"If so Moonpool protected us from them before, why will she not now? No the attack will come from either the Romans or one of the other races in that part of the world and even with her aid we cannot defeat them."

"You said she told you she had certain powers."

"She also told me she had no authority over the wills of people."

"And the Son? Surely he has authority?"

"I do not know what he will do. I have prayed but have had no answer."

"I feel so powerless, I wish I had the strength of my ancestors."

"But would any of them have been able to stop such an invasion? The whole world is a different place now, for good and for bad. It is us who face this and we will have to do what we can."

Idwal sighed. "Then we must seek for peace."

Aderyn stood before the altar in the sanctuary just before the sun rose after the longest night. A bowl of coals was burning. The people were all gathered behind her. The air was still, the sky clear and brightening in the east and a frost lay on the ground.

"Over many generations our people have gathered here to pray that the sun might rise and grow in strength again." She called in a loud voice. "Now we know that it was a picture of the birth of The Son Of The Maker Of All Things. Jeshua, Son of God born into our world, the rising and setting and rising again of the sun a picture of his death and rising to life again. As the sun rises we celebrate his birth and his resurrection."

The sky brightened in the east as the flash of the sun appeared over the hill yet the people remained silent.

"Oh Jeshua, you have entered our world and have shown your love for us. Lighten our darkness and protect us in the uncertain days to come."

I felt her doubt, I felt her reaching out to me as the one certainty in her changing world for she had not seen the Son but had seen me. If only he would show himself to people for their faith is so fragile. I daren't reach back, it was not my place.

The sun rose to appear in full above the hill. The fire in the bowl flared suddenly. I felt a familiar presence and she must have too.

She turned to the people. "He has heard our prayer, when the enemy comes he will be with us so that we will not be destroyed. Yet we must seek for peace, this he has told me."

The people cheered as they had every year since this event had been celebrated here. But despite their enthusiastic cheering there remained some doubt in their hearts. Was it because they didn't yet know the Son or was it because they were expected to seek peace with the newcomers rather than be spared invasion?

Not all the people believed I existed, not many acknowledged The Maker Of All Things. Some had received the message of Branok with joy and they would gather with Aderyn to pray and to talk but as yet there was very little information and so much was still speculation and stories. Branok had only told her some of the stories and she wanted to know so much more.

But at least they were here at this holy place even if only for traditions sake or for the festivities after.

In either case, the party was as full of joy as it ever was. The pig roasting on the spit, the wine more easily available flowed freely. The dancing with the stringed instruments and the horns and drums continued all day. Everyone forgot the cold and the possible threat of invasion, today was all that mattered and today was a celebration.

Aderyn came back once everyone had drifted away from the party as the sun began to sink in the west.

"Moonpool." She said softly. "I so wanted you to appear but I am glad you didn't, you are so much wiser than I am, you know what is right. I don't know how hard it is for you to hold back, for so long you have been the one we worshipped here."

I stood with her.

"It is not hard. I am only a servant and this place is a thin place where the two worlds are close to each other, therefore it is a place that draws people to worship as it draws me for peace and solitude, I should not be worshipped. Also, it is not my place to interfere. In the past perhaps I have got too involved but a piece of friendly advice to you humans now and then can't hurt.

You have such short lives and have to learn over and again the lessons of the past while I do have some experience."

She turned to me, took my right hand with her left and patted it with her right. "You I can see and touch and talk with. It is hard to have faith all the time, The Maker Of All Things has never made it easy and it is not easy with his Son. To trust without seeing."

"You have a depth of faith you do not know or you would not have seen me either. But be assured The Maker Of All Things does have a plan and his Son is with you. You fear the future. But the future is only tomorrow's today."

As the earth rolled on Aderyn kept her faith. At times when life was hard and she had her doubts the best I could do was assure her that all Branok had said was true.

"Every day we step into the future." I said. "You must be strong for yourself, but more importantly you must be strong for Idwal and for the people. And, for Idwal's son."

"Idwal hasn't …"

"His wife is expecting."

CHAPTER 4

Marcus Quasitor

The earth rolled on and on, many seasons came and went, each year they celebrated the life, death and life of the Son and hoped beyond hope there would be no invasion. But when the news came they knew it was only a matter of time.

Morgan son of Idwal had gathered the elders of the villages of the valley together and a large number of fighting men, and they stood at the eastern end of the valley where the road came over the hill above the narrowest part of the valley. They had reports of the Roman invasion, the resistance, and the violent bloodshed. They had heard that they had overrun Môrdun and had set up a camp in what they now called Mordunum. Having defeated the Chieftain of the west the land was now theirs so what was left for Morgan and his people?

"Remember." He said to the men. "We may defeat the first group, but there will be others. If it comes to fighting we will do our best but we will be in danger of losing everything. These Romans will take without concern for our people. We must bow to them and hope their leader will listen if we are to have peace. I know it will be hard but when they come no one move, let them strike the first blow."

Five and four horsemen rode into view bearing the standard of the 2nd Augustian Legion. Morgan and the elders stood their ground with their swords and shields in their hands. The riders came close and stopped just before them, no one spoke. The horses stamped and blew but the riders sat impassive, tense, unsure.

Even as spirit I am only at one place at any time so I stood unseen between them, only the horses were aware of me and I could calm them at least. I spoke to the mind of the horse that bore the leader and I read there that his master was a kind man and although he would fight if necessary he would prefer not to and this gave me hope. His master wondered at the sudden peace of his horse and took his eyes off Morgan for a moment and looked in my direction, he couldn't see me but did he catch that glimpse out of the corner of his eye in the way that humans do before their rational mind dismisses it?

I whispered to Morgan that this was a man who could be trusted and although he would fight actually preferred peace and I hoped Morgan was open enough to hear without knowing where the thought came from. Morgan had a choice, they could fight these men and probably defeat them this time but more would come and he could not fight an unstoppable force or he could listen to the voice in his head and seek peace and hope they would be spared. If there was peace then his people would survive and perhaps in time there would come a chance to beat them. He also knew of the advice I had given Aderyn to reason with them or be swept away.

To my relief Morgan lay down his arms and the elders and their followers followed suit.

"I am Morgan ap Idwal and I relinquish command of the valley to you." He shouted up at the leader.

He in turn dismounted and picked up Morgan's sword.

"I am Marcus Quasitor. I accept your offer Morgan ap Idwal, you are a man of wisdom and foresight. Take you sword." He handed it back to Morgan. "I have come to offer terms and you are a man of peace with whom I can do business."

Morgan took his sword in stunned silence. This was not what he expected from what he had heard of the Romans and it was more than he hoped for.

"Then come, eat, and we will talk."

Leading the way to Sarnlas Morgan instructed some of his men to look after the horses and some of Marcus' men, while Marcus and his second in command and two of his own men were taken into the large round house that was specifically for meetings. Aderyn, now old and grey and quite frail, was already waiting, I was standing invisibly behind her.

Bread, cheese, cold meats and ale were brought in.

"Morgan ap Idwal, I thank you for your willingness to talk and your hospitality." Began Marcus.

"Likewise, I am grateful for your willingness to talk, I have heard what you have done across the country."

"The Empire wishes to civilise the world, its methods can be rather extreme. I am merely an agent of the Emperor but I do have the freedom to expand Rome's influence any way I choose, I would rather choose to talk rather than fight."

"And we have little choice, accept or die."

"Such is the Empire I am afraid."

"And what do you propose?"

"This valley is a day's march from Mordunum and another day's march to the coast. All I need is an outpost here. It needn't be here but anywhere within the valley. We will keep away from your people and I can appoint you as local chieftain and you can run your affairs as you always have. Apart from troops passing through we do not need to have much to do with each other."

Morgan looked across at Aderyn.

Silently she asked me, 'Is this a reasonable solution?'

'It is, you will not get a better one.'

She nodded to Morgan.

Morgan then turned to his men and spoke to them in Celtic.

"Do we accept this offer? Do you think the people can live with this?""

"Do we have a choice? At least, as you say, we can live with this, I fear the alternative. Even if we hold them off many people will die."

"You both agree?"

"Yes, Morgan, but let us hope they do leave us alone."

"How do you know you can trust me?" Mogan asked Marcus reverting to Latin.

"How do you know you can trust me? Neither of us knows for certain but for the moment it is a good deal, if either of us breaks the trust we will have to deal with the consequences then."

Once all the details had been worked out Marcus came to the holy place where Morgan's cousin Carwen was tending the flame that continually burned on the altar.

"You must be Carwen." He said as he entered the enclosure. "I am Marcus."

"I know who you are." She replied coolly without turning.

"You are not happy with my being here."

"Am I supposed to be?"

"It is the way of things. The whole world belongs to us now."

"I don't think it belongs to you. You are just passing through as so many people have before."

Carwen had been introduced to me by her mother Aderyn after her training which now incorporated the new teaching of the Son with the old ways. When she knew the Romans were coming she asked me about all the comings and goings of people right back to the days of Ban and understood my perspective on the passing of time and people.

"We are not like so many people before, we are the modern world and we sweep all the old ways away. We bring civilisation and wonderful technologies."

She turned to him and looked him up and down. He had a sort of presence but he was not a cruel or hard man. He was a soldier in a chain of command.

"Are you a religious man Marcus Quasitor?"

"I accept the gods of my people and I am expected to accept the gods of the people we conquer because this is important for stability."

"That is not what I asked. I didn't ask if the commander of the Roman scouting party accepted the religions of his people and the indigenous people he conquered. I asked if you were a religious man."

He smiled. "I am a practical man, so I suppose that means I am not religious."

She stood and looked at him long and hard, trying to sum him up. She reached out to me.

In her thoughts she asked me, 'Moonpool, could you appear before him?'

'To what end?'

'If he is going to set up a staging post here he needs to know about you.'

'No, he doesn't need to know about me, all land is overseen and the Romans will do their own thing without acknowledging us.'

"So." Said Marcus, breaking into her silent thoughts. "Whose temple is this? Who is your local god?"

"Ah that is two different questions. This is a temple to The Maker Of All Things and to his Son. Pwll'euad is the spirit of the valley and she doesn't like the term goddess."

"I beg her pardon. Pwll'euad, we have no Roman equivalent. I'm no scholar but I don't think Luna Stagnum would do her justice, neither would Selene Minor after the goddess of the moon. Why does she have that name? There is no pool here, there is a river."

"There was a lake once, long ago, and the first settler here saw the moon reflected in the surface of the lake."

"A reflection of the moon, then she is Luna Imago. There is still no Roman equivalent. I will have a word with some of our learned men as we do like to include your local deities. But the first settler seeing the moon's reflection, this must be a very old legend."

"She is not a deity. She is the spirit of the valley. We worship the Son here. And the story of the first settler is not a legend, Pwll'euad herself told me."

He smiled at this and a slight memory of an almost glimpse while he sat on his horse earlier stirred in his mind. "The Son, the moon's reflection, as I said I am a practical man so it is all the same to me. You continue to do what you do here and I will not interfere, we have come to bring many things that will bring you into the modern world but you may keep your devotions. You will find us more reasonable than you have been led to believe, we are a civilised people."

Carwen looked at him steadily, trying to weigh him up. No he was not what she expected.

She stayed after he left. I knew she wanted to talk so I stood beside her.

"You know your own business, Moonpool, and I suppose I understand. I just wish sometimes either you or the Son would make things a little easier."

"Marcus may say he is not religious but I got the impression he glimpsed me on the road, he is more spiritual than he realises or is willing to admit. I thought you needed to know this as it may be something to remember in your dealings with him."

"He glimpsed you?"

"Humans let their rational minds get in the way and they don't see what they learn not to see."

After some time she asked. "The Romans are the people you warned us about. This is the violent change."

"Yes, and the first meeting has gone well, it will be a change but fortunately not a violent one. It will not be easy and many people will not accept it but there can be peace under the Romans, even I don't know how long they will be here. I have seen so many changes and so many people come and go. When the Celts came you became one people and this may happen again. Humans are resilient, you will live with whatever happens."

"And you?"

"This is a different world now. I will be needed less and less. In time I will be completely forgotten and I will fall asleep."

"That will be a dark day for the valley."

Strangely I was alright with this. I knew I would never be human and I had lost so many friends over the ages. This at least would be an end.

CHAPTER 5

Roman Occupation

Marcus and his men camped in temporary shelters they had brought with them in the flat area behind the temple. Early the next day he came to the sanctuary to watch the sun rise and he just stood there silently. Surprisingly for a man who had known violence his mind was quite calm.

"This is a peaceful place, it reminds me of home." He sighed. I do not know who he was talking to, perhaps just to himself. "I know I have a job to do and I do not believe I will succeed."

Later he took some of his men and they began to scout about for a suitable permanent site. From the original track that led from the temple, past Pentreban and up the hill he reached the wooden road. He crossed the road and branched right across fields and followed the valley to a hill well away from other settlements.

"Here is the place we will build." He said to his men. "It is away from everyone. I don't think we will have trouble but you can never be too sure. Darius, take two men and ride back to Mordunum. Tell them we have peacefully settled a day's march from there and need engineers and labourers."

Many of the labourers were men from Mordunum. Although there was much work to do there Darius felt that since they had an outpost this far west the capital wasn't in such imminent danger and these men could be spared.

Marcus and Darius found a hill where they could look down on the work on the stockade and much of the road that went on into the west.

"We cannot rest here for long." Said Marcus. "The west is where the danger lies. We have come further than we hoped in the time and our forces are at full stretch. I will need to continue on and find out just how far raiders from Hibernia have come."

"Won't the local people resist them?"

"As they see it they have the Hibernians on one side and us on the other so what choice do they have. They cannot fight on both sides so perhaps they will wait until we meet in the middle and let us fight it out ourselves. Our aim is to spread out into Hibernia eventually but we do not have the men to do it yet. We had hoped to train up local warriors with our modern tactics but we do not have the time and they are reluctant to fight for us."

"We could always dig in and hold out here and let them stretch themselves too far."

"That would be sensible but Rome is not always sensible. Safe in their own country they believe the world belongs to them already and is theirs for the taking. The report has gone back that we are this close and I will soon receive orders to continue west."

Once the stockade was built work began on the roads. Darius was promoted to commander of the garrison and already soldiers were arriving from the east. Marcus came to the temple one last time before he left, he stood in silence for a while, deep in thought.

"Maybe I am talking to myself, but this so reminds me of my home and there I could talk into the open air like here and feel that nature itself was listening."

I was tempted to appear to him, there was enough belief from Aderyn, Morgan and Carwen for me to take on human form. But somehow this would spoil his mood, he simply needed to talk.

"I know I will die on this next mission, I wish I could send a message home. Maybe the wind can carry my love to my family."

I didn't know where his family were but I spoke to the winds and a strong wind blew suddenly down the valley and away to the west. Maybe the winds would find his family. He looked wistfully down the valley following the wind.

Then jumping onto his horse he rode back to the road and set out west with his scouting party replacing Darius with another man to make up the five and four horsemen. Although I felt for Marcus, a much more open and spiritually aware man than Darius and as such could have been an asset to the people here, I was no longer concerned with him but I knew he ran into opposition from raiders from Erin taking advantage of the unsettled state of the peninsula.

The Romans are very industrious and organised and as time passed they built their stone road on top of the wooden one. However from here they only got part of the way to the coast because of the raids. From news I had from my cousins the skirmishes they fought gained neither side any ground and for the moment my valley knew peace.

Morgan often came to the temple. He was a devout follower of the Son but he would also come and talk to me from time to time. Humans find dealing directly with the Son rather overawing and prefer to talk to beings closer to themselves and someone they can talk to face to face.

"Pwll'euad you were right. If we had resisted at first they would have had the strength to defeat us, not with the first group perhaps but soon. As it is their power is already fading so perhaps we won't have to put up with them for too long. From what I hear they do not have the strength to drive onward to the coast, soon perhaps we can take back our land unless they are driven back but then we will have raiders from Erin to contend with. We are caught in the middle."

"The world has changed already." I replied. "In my experience time never goes backwards, and do not underestimate the resolve of the Romans and they may be rather stretched they still have many resources. And you are wise not to assume the people from Erin will be any better. Things will never be what they were and the Roman influence will be with us for a long time."

"And what about the Son, surely he will not allow such a cruel people to continue."

"It is not my place to say what the Son Of The Maker Of All Things will do."

"You are spirit so you must know more than I do."

"I am still a created being and I don't think even the angels know his plans."

"But his message of peace and hope should be changing the world by now."

"You humans are slow and stubborn and proud and arrogant. Remember they killed the Son, they will not all listen to his message."

"We are not all like that."

"No indeed, the majority are good and kind and honest and it is that in humanity that draws me back rather than turning away. The Son Of The Maker Of All Things has told me I still have a part to play, so I stay."

"And will you protect us?"

"I will do what I can, also what I am allowed. I do not know the future so I cannot promise anything."

"But at least you are here."

Life settled down under the Romans. It became obvious that I wasn't going to help drive them out and neither was the Son. The temple became dedicated to Selene, the name they gave to Silverwheel, by the wisdom of their religious leaders and I was forgotten. Worship there was a strange mix of Roman meaningless ceremony and appeasement of imagined gods and actual nature spirits who had got above themselves in distant lands because of the Romans and those who had accepted their ways, even their devotion to Selene bore little resemblance to the spirit I knew, and then there was simple Christian prayer and the sharing of bread and wine at times when the others weren't there by the small group who followed the way of the Son. Darius turned a blind eye to the latter even though the Druids had been outlawed and many of them slaughtered in the north. The seasons came and went as the earth continued to roll through space, Darius was replaced, generation passed to generation and I was forgotten, even by the small group who worshipped the Son in secret.

Trade was good and the people thrived. Occasionally the raiders from Erin caused trouble and troops came from Moridunum to drive them back but they had gained a foothold in the west that the Romans couldn't spare the troops to drive back completely. They had always intended to invade Erin but were fighting battles on too many fronts not least among themselves.

CHAPTER 6

Hard Decisions

The earth rolled on, unaffected by forces of humans. The land still went through her seasons and continued to produce fruit and grain and cared not who was in charge. Thaddeus was put in charge of what had now become simply a trading post. He saw no reason to isolate himself from the indigenous people, after all they had taken on many of the Roman ways, so he built a modest, by Roman standards, villa just along the valley from Prentre ban. Although he called himself Governor he was really only a business man and trader. However he was a devout follower of the Way as the followers of the Son now were called. And although it was strictly illegal he had built a special room in his villa for the faithful to meet once a week.

He still attended the rituals of the Romans in Selene's temple for show because of his position. He also occasionally came to the temple early in the morning just for the peace and solitude.

"I know there is a presence here." He said into the air. "There is a presence in the valley. I have always lived in large towns but I heard stories of spirits in the countryside. This is my first posting to the countryside and I can feel you."

Unexpectedly he reached out to me. His mind was very open. He was also a good and kind man. I was drawn to appear but he was a follower of the Way and I might confuse him.

"Our Lord said that if the people kept silent the stones would cry out. The psalmist says the trees of the field shall clap their hands. The glory of God is everywhere and there is life in everything."

If only the Maker of All Things would say something. Would it be wrong to appear to him? There was no need, to appear to him would be for myself and not for him.

"Ah well." He sighed. "Perhaps I am wrong but there is a definite presence here."

Thaddeus was well liked by the local people. He made a point of getting to know Maelog, grandson of Morgan, and his family. Although Maelog had no official status he was still understood locally as the chieftain. This was not merely a political move to keep the local people happy for the two of them had a lot in common and were great friends.

"Maelog, I have a question and I don't know if you will think me stupid in asking." He asked in Celtic.

They were in Maelog's round house sampling some fine wine Thaddeus had brought in specially.

"What is it?"

The question was a long time coming. Maelog waited and Thaddeus considered how to broach the subject. Eventually Thaddeus spoke again.

"How long have we known each other? Three, four years? Can I ask a strange question? If it is a stupid question then let us both laugh and then forget it."

Maelog smiled but remained silent.

Thaddeus rolled the wine round in his cup for some time. Then, having decided looked directly at Maelog.

"We are both followers of the Way but sometimes I feel there is a presence in the valley."

Maelog looked at his friend, unsure where this was going. Having always lived here he felt nothing unusual in the valley, it was simply his home and it was beautiful and peaceful.

"Not a malevolent presence but a presence of goodness and peace."

"God has blessed our valley. We are at peace here, and I must admit it is because of your people and you, personally are good to us. The raiders have not yet come this far, and we have your people to thank for that."

Thaddeus took a long draught of wine before continuing.

"I know the presence of God and I have often felt Jesus himself among us. No this is something else, something of the earth, something of the valley itself."

Maelog smiled and took a sip of wine, then looked vaguely into the centre of the house.

"We have our legends." He said quietly, smiling to himself. "My ancestors believed in a spirit of the valley. But surely we know better now, we have outgrown superstitions. This is simply a beautiful valley with a long history and it is easy to imagine things. My ancestors didn't fully understand so they filled nature with gods and spirits."

"Yes, I know all that. But still, I wonder. Did the spirit of the valley have a name?"

"You are serious aren't you." Maelog looked searchingly at him. "Let us go back to it being a stupid question. There is only one God."

"You are right, it is a stupid question."

They both laughed and the subject was dropped.

Later that evening Thaddeus said his goodnights and left.

"If you see Carys send her home, it is late." Maelog shouted as he left.

But Carys was waiting outside for him. Carys would soon be a woman, she was already a good horsewoman and quite fearless. She was tall and dark and in many ways reminded me of Ban's daughter Moonpool who he named after me.

"Carys ..." Thaddeus began quite loudly.

"Hush." She put her finger to her lips then waited to hear if there were stirrings from inside.

"Carys." Thaddeus whispered. "Your father wants you to come in, it is getting late."

"I heard your conversation when I came by earlier so I came back to see you. Don't tell anyone I told you this but her name is Pwll'euad."

"You know her then?"

"I wish I did, I only know the legends." She looked sad at this. "If you find her, tell her I would like to see her."

He could see she was in earnest.

"What do the legends say about her?"

"She was here when there was a lake in the valley, I have heard that she was given her name because the moon was reflected in the lake. It is said that she used to fight our enemies."

He thought for a moment. "But she has not fought against us coming here."

"Perhaps she doesn't see you as an enemy."

"But we are invaders and we fought many battles with the people of this island."

"Your people maybe, but not you."

They both reflected in silence for a while and Thaddeus wondered at her last statement.

"Thank you for that but let us keep it to ourselves. Your father would not approve and as followers of the Way it may be seen as blasphemous."

She smiled at him. "We are romantics and there is no harm in romanticism."

That evening Carwen, Maelog's cousin, came to his house. Maelog could see he was angry.

"You don't like me talking to Thaddeus do you." Maelog said.

"Should I? I don't know how you can be all over him like you are. He is our jailer, we have no freedom or authority ourselves. You are only his pet dog."

"The Romans leave us alone and we leave them alone, we get on with life. You are doing well trading with them."

"That is different, it is business not personal."

"So, what am I supposed to do? They are here, we have to live with it."

"Not everyone wants to live with it. You should be chieftain but the people don't talk to you, not when you are in his house half the time. The people talk to me, I am more of a chieftain than you are."

"You do not speak for everyone, I know people have still not accepted them but they would rather peaceful lives than conflict."

"I saw Carys talking to him outside, she is only a girl. You need to watch them, these Romans have no scruples, they take what they want."

Maelog looked over at Carys sleeping the other side of the house.

"I have warned you." Carwen whispered. "I can do no more. Listen to the people and look to your daughter."

With that he stormed out. The arrow had struck home and Maelog was left with questions.

The little stone hut that Gwybod had built so long ago still stood but it had been neglected and ivy had taken hold. No one ever went there. I found that there was enough belief in me, possibly Carys or even Thaddeus, that I could take on human form so I sat by the stone hut and looked down into the valley. So much had changed, the signs of Roman occupation were there such as square buildings rather than round and the stone road running through the valley, but there was still so much that hadn't. Humans tend to think of the Moon only being in the sky at night but she was overhead now, very close to the sun from the earth's perspective and therefore invisible. I sought Arianrhos.

"Silverwheel." I spoke her old name.

She came, silver and mysterious as ever.

"Moonpool." She used my old name.

"We have had no instructions, no do's and don'ts. I know Thaddeus believes I exist and for some reason wants to see me. He is a follower of the Way and therefore I feel it would be wrong for me to appear to him."

"I am Selene to many people now. I have this demand to be seen all the time. Should I appear?"

"But he has some hard decisions. Should I help or just keep watch?"

We looked at each other. I sighed.

"You believe it would be wrong." She said. "You have answered your question."

I looked around. I may have accepted who and what I am but I missed the feelings of the human form and I missed the sights and sounds I have when in this form. I also missed human contact, I missed human friends even if their lives are so short.

"There is nothing wrong with sitting here when no one is about though." I said more as a statement than a question.

"This is a nice spot. The Moon is so bleak, perhaps I will sit with you from time to time."

We sat silently for a while, there seemed to be a sadness about her.

"Are you sad, Silverwheel?"

"The Romans called your holy place Selene after me rather than you. Apart from Carys you are nearly forgotten, and Thaddeus would acknowledge you. I suppose I am sad because you may fall asleep. I nearly lost you once before and felt so helpless. Oh, Moonpool please don't fall asleep, please promise you will stay, I know it is a lot to ask."

"It is not a lot to ask. I can't think I have finished with interfering yet, not for a long time."

We held each other for a while until the moon moved away and Silverwheel had to move with it.

"Besides." I said to no one, or was it The Maker Of All Things. "I want to be remembered."

Chapter 7

The Underground

It was early in the morning, the sun had not yet risen but the sky was beginning to brighten. Carwyn stood on the bridge over the Taf, watching the road for any sign of anyone stirring this early. He was very closed up in himself, he had a lot of hate and resentment, and I knew he was up to something. Not because I was deliberately watching out for him but because Maelog was worried and had been trying to find out who he was mixing with and what sort of things he had been saying. He knew he had been stirring dissention but there was quite a lot of that anyway, many people were not comfortable with the Roman presence. I cannot watch everything but I had become aware of signs that were being passed from person to person as if some secret was being shared and these secrets always led back to Carwyn. So today I watched him.

Carwyn was a successful trader and he did well by sending carts between Mordunum and the west. But it was more than trade. For although he was doing very well because of the Roman occupation he had an intense dislike for them and was part of an organisation in touch with the people of Erin, sending information about Roman strengths, weaknesses and movements and bringing weapons back to use against them.

A cart arrived from the west and turned off the road to the track that came down to the bridge. The cart paused before it came to the bridge and turned back. A man slipped out from under the coverings, a hooded cloak pulled close about him.

"Cathal." Carwyn said softly. "Come, we need to talk away from prying eyes."

Without speaking the two of them went up to Gwybod's hut. There was barely enough room inside for both of them so they sat outside on some large stones that had fallen from the hut and gazed down at the valley where the people were just stirring.

"Well, what news from Mordunum?" Asked Cathal throwing back his hood, he was a slender wiry man with a shock of red hair and a thick beard.

"Rome has sent no extra troops, they don't keep a large force there because the Romans keep many of the people happy as they are quite well off and they are amused by the plays and the games in the amphitheatre the Romans built. There is certainly unrest among the poorer people but they have little influence. Our men try to persuade people to turn on the oppressor but it is hard when they don't feel oppressed. We do have a following among the poorer people and have persuaded some of them to accept weapons and wait for a signal from us. But so many people see the occupiers as civilised, improving their lives, while they see you as savages and barbarians."

"Roman lies."

"I am afraid that is the way of things, when people are comfortable they believe what they are told."

"And what of beyond Mordunum?"

"There are uprisings but they are quashed quickly and harshly. It seems the Romans are here to stay. Reports from Rome do talk of political infighting but the empire is greater than just Rome itself."

"And here? What of Thaddeus and Maelog?"

"Maelog can't see that he is only a puppet and thinks of Thaddeus as a friend, I have tried to sow seeds of doubt and suspicion." He scowled. "They get on well and have no idea of my special work, we are free to do as we wish right under their noses, Maelog trusts me so Thaddeus has no reason to be suspicious. Much as I hate to admit it if something happened to Thaddeus a new governor would be appointed who might be inclined to be more watchful and that would be bad for our cause."

"As you wish."

"If you had sufficient men you could easily take the fortress here and probably even be able to drive on to Mordunum itself for they have become soft. Do you have a force large enough for that?"

"I could get a force but not quite large enough to take the fortress here, if you have enough men to help we could possibly do that, and then we could hold out here. Oh that we were one united people but we are not, we fight among ourselves still and I fear that if the Romans decided to come in force we do not have the unity to stop them. The best we can hope for is to make them think it is too much trouble and keep them at bay. Maybe, with luck we could drive them back to Mordunum for the moment and then possibly persuade other tribes that we have the strength to defeat them if only we could fight together."

As he rose to go he reached into his belt for a small sack. "Here, I have the poisons you asked for, can you be sure they will get into the food supply of Romans in Mordunum only?"

"No, there are those who are all over the Romans and do well out of them. But then if they take that risk they will suffer the consequences."

"Good enough. I go south now, there are other peoples in this world than the Romans if only they would work together." He sighed. "That is their only strength these Romans, they may not all be from Rome but they are organised in ways no one else is."

Carwyn sat for some time looking down into the valley. He didn't acknowledge the Son or even me. The Son would not interfere with the dealings of the humans so I was powerless to do so as well. I wanted to warn Thaddeus which I could have done but that would take interfering too far. It is so frustrating when you see and hear such things and can tell no one.

I did wonder if I could at least interfere with the contents of the sack, I worked out what herbs and plants and fungi it contained.

'Oh Maker Of All Things, I know this sort of thing is common all over the world but you have made me guardian of the valley and I would so much like to keep peace here.'

Silence. I could not speak to SIlverwheel, the moon was the other side of the earth and she had concerns there.

At mid-day Carwen was overseeing the loading of a wagon for Mordunum. Produce had been brought in from local farms, cured meat, cheeses, wheat for flour.

As the driver climbed up onto the wagon Carwen handed him the sack he had received from Cathal.

"Special delicacies from the west. Make sure you give it to Elwyn personally, he is waiting for it."

The driver nodded, then took up the reins.

"And safe journey." Carwen gave the horse a slap on the rump and the wagon rolled off.

I did think of stopping the horse.

'Leave her go.' Came a familiar voice and I knew The Maker Of All Things knew things I didn't.

So I simply watched them go.

Thaddeus was suddenly ill for a few days though I could not sense any illness, and this was not my doing. However this prevented him from going to Mordunum which meant that when a serious malady affected the troops stationed there, many of the high ranking Romans and some of their friends he was not there. It was reported that many of the Romans died as well as local people who were close to them and in the confusion the people of Erin saw an opportunity.

Chapter 8

Battle Prevented

A cold wind blew from the west as Carwyn stood at the point where the spur road to the outpost left the main road. He had gathered a small band together armed with the swords and spears they had received from Erin and they lay hidden in the trees and bushes a little further up the lane that lead northwards to the many farmsteads that dotted the countryside. He daren't gather too many because the more people who knew about his plans the more likely he would be found out, and besides, despite what Carwen claimed, Maelog was highly respected even though he was friendly with Thaddeus and very few would go against him.

Carwyn had been informed that a force was coming from the East. They planned to take over the outpost before regrouping with as many local men as they could gather and, if enough people could be drawn to their cause, stage an all-out attack on Mordunum while they had the advantage.

The men lay hidden in the dark of the night, waiting, expectant. Carwyn paced up and down, glancing occasionally along the road to the west, no sign of the warriors coming from there yet, but mostly keeping his eye on the spur to the outpost. He didn't think they would send a sentry down to the junction to keep watch, they rarely did, but with the situation in Mordunum they might think it necessary.

He had been right to keep watch for he heard the tramp of marching feet in time to hide himself in the bushes. Two guards carrying a lamp marched to the junction and stopped. They looked around but the light of the lamp didn't penetrate far into the dark, and because they had a lamp there eyes could make out nothing beyond its light.

After some time they just stood there, it didn't look as if they intended to return. Carwyn reasoned that they would be there for some time and wouldn't be expected to report back unless they saw something. He and his men could dispose of them easily and no one would know until more came to relieve them, they could dispose of them too but when the first two didn't return those in the outpost would become suspicious. He tried to reckon on the number in the outpost. They could kill these two and the next two and although he could not storm the outpost himself he hoped the men from Erin would soon be along and surely there would be enough. He would be happier if he knew how many would be coming, and how soon they would come, but he had to do something now.

As quietly as possible he crept closer to his men and silently got them to understand his plan. All at once they broke cover and the Romans immediately took a defensive stand but the surprise sudden onslaught meant it wasn't in time. Swords were drawn, the clash of metal on metal, and soon it was over. They quickly killed the Roman soldiers but one of Carwyn's men was seriously wounded in the shoulder and had to be carried into the bushes.

They dragged the bodies off the road and hid them as best they could in a short time, and put out the lamp. Then Carwyn separated his men on either side of the spur.

Two things I knew soon after this, riders from the west had just entered the valley but probably not as many as Carwyn had hoped for, also a large number of Romans marching from the east had also entered the valley. Although the Romans were on foot the distance was much shorter and they would probably all arrive at the same time. Because the force from the east were on horseback they would have a slight advantage but not enough, their attack would fail because they were too few and I have seen enough bloodshed to not want it to happen again. So how could I stop it? I could not warn Carwyn, he would not hear me.

I could warn Carys but I didn't want her involved. I couldn't warn Maelog because he didn't believe I existed. Thaddeus may have heard but how would he treat Carwyn and the other villagers with him? So I did what I could and hoped The Maker Of All Things would forgive me.

In my natural state I can be in nature so I could reach out to all the animals. All the dogs in the area suddenly started barking and howling, all the wild animals started running about in and out where the men were hiding, and all the night birds swooped and called and squeeked and hooted. I could be in the trees and the trees swayed wildly as if blown by a gale even though the wind was not that strong, their branches creaking, the leaves shaking and rustling. I could reach down deep into the earth and the ground shook and threw everyone off balance.

"This is a bad omen Carwyn!" Shouted one of the men.

"We can't stay here. There is some evil at work." Shouted another.

"The gods are angry." Shouted another.

But then the Romans approached from one side and the riders from Erin from the other. The sky in the east was beginning to brighten but nature had put everyone into confusion and for a while no one moved, trying to stand upright despite the shaking of the earth.

Carwyn jumped up from his hiding place and quickly summed up the situation in an instant, quite apart from the violence of nature. There were just not nearly enough from Erin even though they were on horseback and his men were too few, for there were too many Romans from Mordunum. They might defeat the Romans by sheer ferocity but it was by no means certain and there would be a heavy loss of life on both sides. Even if they defeated the Romans here they could get no further and they would not be able to storm the fortress that would still be heavily guarded, and the fact that so many had come from Mordunum probably meant there was a greater force there now that he hadn't reckoned with. The plan was doomed to fail.

"The gods are against us, stay where you are." He shouted to the horsemen in Celtic. Then in the best Latin he could manage he shouted to the Romans. "You have angered the gods of the land, come no further."

The wildness of nature round them brought fear to them all.

Carwyn also suddenly realised that the sudden violence of nature mean that I existed and because of this his belief enabled me to appear, which I did. I was so worked up that I appeared twice my normal size and with my huge wings outstretched.

"This is sacred ground, you shall not fight, you shall not spill blood." I boomed.

In the grey of the predawn I probably appeared more ominous than in the full light of day. Everyone stood their ground for a moment, Carwyn's men fled into the countryside, then the force from Erin wheeled their horses round and galloped back the way they had come. I kept my stand between Carwyn and the Romans giving him enough time to retreat into the trees. As the sun began to rise I faded away leaving the Romans stunned and with no one to fight, and not sure what I would do they made their way to the outpost.

Carwyn knew that there would be need to answer for the two dead Romans so later that day he went to Maelog.

"Maelog." He said kneeling before Maelog who was just coming out of his house.

"Carwyn, there is no need to kneel."

He remained kneeling, laying his sword on the ground. "I give myself up into your hands to do as you wish. I organised an attack last night with some of our people and a force from Erin on the Roman outpost. I killed two of the guards but Pwll'eauad appeared and stopped us, she also stopped a force from Mordunum so thanks to her there wasn't any more bloodshed. I don't think any of our people would have survived otherwise.

I take full responsibility and do not want any of our people to be punished."

"Ah. That accounts for the animals and the trees and the shaking of the ground." He thought for a moment. "Carwyn, if I hand you over to Thaddeus he will have to take you to Mordunum where you will be tried and executed. If you run the Romans will pursue you unless you leave now before they set out, the only place you would be safe is Erin because they cannot get there. Will you be able to get passage there?"

Carwyn nodded.

Maelog continued. "I do not want to know who else was involved and I haven't seen you."

Carwyn stood slowly.

"You had better have been gone already." Maelog said quietly as he turned to go back into the house.

Carwyn paused for a moment and in that moment Maelog turned back and embraced him.

"Do you think they will accept you in Erin? I will miss you cousin Carwyn."

"Yes I have friends there. I will miss you too and all the people here."

Maelog turned and went back into the house and Carwyn made good his escape, I know he did make it to Erin but what sort of reception he had I do not know.

"You are a good man." Said Thaddeus as Maelog sat down the other side of the low table.

"He is my cousin."

"And he is a brave man. He could have just gone. But by coming here first he has saved your villages."

They both picked up their wine and reflected for a time.

"I had always heard Pwll'euad was a peaceful spirit. I had no idea she could do what she did last night." Mused Thaddeus.

"Nor I. There are legends of her fighting for the people before but I thought she was only a legend. So much for your question being stupid the other day, and so much for our beliefs."

"It is a different story that I heard from the Centurion. He returned to Mordunum and reported that he had routed the attackers with much bloodshed and that apart from the loss of two of the soldiers from the outpost there were no casualties on his side. I go to Mordunum tomorrow and will be asking questions, what shall I ask?"

"Ask him why he didn't pursue the invaders and inform him they have all fled back to Hibernia. I dare say he will not want to pursue them and will not give a reason. He is going to wonder about all our local gods. My only hope is that although he has such a strong force he will not decide to press on towards the west."

"I can arrange for him and his men to be transferred to some other front to the north."

"And what of the mysterious deaths in Mordunum?"

"There were no deaths. A lot of people had a mysterious illness, the rumour of deaths they put about was a trap. They have their spies too and Carwyn's plan was known about."

They were both silent for a while, deep in thought.

"I am still confused." Admitted Maelog. "With the coming of the Son weren't the old gods, even if they ever existed, supposed to be gone?"

I sat with Silverwheel by Gwybod's old hut.

"I am in trouble now." I said.

"Has he said anything?"

"Not yet."

"Then you are not in trouble. We may be spirit but we are nature as well and because of that we are closer to the humans than the angels. We cannot help but get involved and your involvement is for the good which is not so of all our kind. If he was going to punish you he would have done so already. Take his silence as a reprimand in itself."

"And as a lesson not to get involved like that again."

"No one has said that." She added with a smile.

Chapter 9

The Missionary

The earth rolled on and on. In time there was no one who believed in me anymore and Silverwheel and I had to make do with talking in our natural form.

Leo first appeared striding along the road in a simple travelling cloak and an iron cross on a thong about his neck and a long staff in his hand. He made his way to the Roman garrison. He showed a parchment to the guard at the entrance who nodded him in.

On entering the governor Titus came to meet him.

Leo offered him the parchment. "I am Leo, I have been sent by the church that has been set up by the Emperor Constantine himself in Rome. I am here to bring good news and to put aside the old pagan practices we followed in our ignorance."

Titus studied the parchment for a while.

"Welcome Leo. I am Titus, governor of the valley and anything you need I will provide. But first, you must be hungry and tired, come you are my guest. We have a small room here, it is a little basic but it is dry and comfortable and I will make sure food is provided."

"A predecessor of mine, Thaddeus, used to hold Christian meetings in his house down in the valley secretly." Titus said during the simple meal they shared. "I use the room for entertaining guests but if you wish I can make it available to you for your ceremonies. I am not a religious man myself but you come with the authority of the emperor so whatever you need is at your disposal."

"Thank you but no, I need a place that is set aside purely for worship. We no longer need to meet in secret but publicly for everyone to see. Is there a temple to the old Roman gods or local gods in the area, where were the public acts of worship that were permitted held?" Asked Leo.

"There is the temple to Selene by the bridge over the river. We had built a small shrine there but we don't use it much, small acts of devotion but no large worship events. We have outgrown our gods, I'm afraid you won't have much interest locally in a new one."

"You do not believe in anything."

"There is no room in our modern world for belief. As I said, I will provide anything you need for your mission because the Emperor commands but my heart is my own."

"Then two things I will ask. Tear down Selene's shrine and build a small wooden hall that will act as a church on the site. Also, I need somewhere simple to live, somewhere out of the way where I may meditate in peace."

"I will get the hall built for you. As for somewhere simple, there is an old stone hut in the hills to the south, probably used by druids when there were such things. People say it is haunted but they often say such things about quiet places. I will have some men take you there tomorrow and if it is suitable I will have it rebuilt as it is probably too small."

"That will suit me fine, something small is all I need."

"You are not from Rome."

"I was not born in Rome if that is what you mean but I have lived in Rome most of my life. I was taken there as a slave but I was given my freedom and I trained in the new church."

Leo was a genuine man of faith and he was very knowledgeable about the life, death and resurrection of the Son. With his simple life in Gwybod's old hut and his walking about the village getting to know people, praying with them in their sufferings and listening to their worries he gained a good following. He walked about the valley breathing in the air, standing for ages looking and listening, drinking in the peace, all as if he was getting to know the valley and how it felt just to be here.

There was already a Christian presence and they were glad to be able worship openly. And in the new church they worshipped the Son with great gladness, and their numbers grew because of his care and understanding.

He dedicated the small church in the old sanctuary site to St Mary, Jesus' mother and would often just stand near the bank where Ban's bones were to watch the sun come up.

"This is an old site." He said into the air rather than to himself, as if he was reaching out to something he didn't know.

I felt strangely drawn to him because as he got to know the valley he got to know me if he did but know it.

"The spirit of this place is not evil."

He was searching with his feelings for something he didn't really understand.

"You are a spirit of peace and good, you are a creature as I am."

He came very close to reaching out to me.

"You are not Selene, but who are you? Are you an angel?"

I wanted to tell him I was not.

He sighed. "It is enough to know you are here. I will have to leave the dedication of the church to St. Mary but I will be glad if you continue to watch over it, as you watch over my hut."

This startled me a little, how did he know Silverwheel and I still met there even though we could not take on physical form. Even now I could not take on physical form for his faith in the spirit of the place was far too vague.

"You know I am not Roman, I was born the other side of Mordunum and I was taken with my parents as slaves to Rome, so I do know our old legends and the deep spirituality of the land."

He breathed deeply, savouring the smells of the land, of the trees and flowers. He listened spellbound to the sound of the river flowing in its course, the birds singing in the trees. He bent down and touched the ground.

"I am home. Here at last I belong."

He stayed there for some time before turning and entering the small church. There he knelt before the small wooden alter and offered prayers to God and to His Son, he thanked God for sending him back here, he prayed for the people of the valley and peace for the world. The Son drew near to him and I was glad.

Too often I had interfered, too often I had got too close. Here was a man I could have come to call a friend if we had met before, but not now. Here was a man I trusted and I was content to slowly fall asleep and disappear, yet I stayed because people come and go and whoever followed him would not be as good. I dearly wanted the Son to tell me what I should do.

Leo sighed, stood slowly and left the church and spoke into the air. "Stay, do not sleep, your work is not finished yet."

This was odd and it took me a moment to work out what it meant. It must have been that the Son had spoken to him and this was a message for me. So, I was to stay then. I did wonder if he had understood the message or simply passed on the words he was asked to say.

As he had asked I watched over the small wooden building that was his church and the stone hut that was his home.

Titus came to the church once as the people were leaving and waited for Leo to come out.

"Titus." Said Leo, pleased to see him. "This is an honour."

"You are a good man, Leo. I hear such good things about you. Would you come to my Villa tomorrow and perhaps we can share a meal and you can tell me something of your faith."

"I would be glad to come."

"I do not promise I will change my belief, but I am curious enough to listen."

So, the next day they shared a simple meal, Leo, Titus, his wife and two boys. And they talked. No, Titus did not change his beliefs but the two did become friends.

Chapter 10

Eochaid Allmuir

The seasons came and the seasons went. A band of raiders from Erin came storming towards the valley. They were taking advantage of the Roman's weakness, aware that some of the troops were leaving Mordunum. They had driven the Romans back this far for the first time and had designs on storming the garrison. Riding at full pelt it was obvious they knew exactly where they were going. There were many men in the band but what they hoped to accomplish attacking the garrison I do not know, unless they also knew that there were only a handful of soldiers left.

But the Romans knew they were coming and they had set up a small guard station at the western edge of my valley. The Governor of Mordunum had brought as many men as he could spare and when they heard the approaching horses they stood across the road.

A long time ago I went with warriors from the valley to help defend them from an attack from Erin and I wondered how the local people would respond to this, but the world had changed so much since then and they were already invaded by the Romans. Maybe they hoped a battle between two rivals would leave them in a stronger position to defend themselves, so waited. I wanted to see how this turned out, I promised myself I would not interfere but there was no harm in watching. I was surprised to find Arberth was there too as his land bordered mine on this side. Obviously no one else would know we were there as we wouldn't have appeared in physical form even if we were able, although I felt the invaders from the west were more in tune with nature and seemed open to the possibility of our existence.

When the riders approached the Romans they halted for the Governor held up his hand.

"I am Quintus Aurelius, Governor of the West." He called out.

"And I am Eochaid Allmuir. I have greater numbers stand aside or we will just ride through you."

"I can see that but before I stand aside I have a proposition to put to you Eochaid Allmuir."

"A proposition? Soon you will all be dead, what need have we for propositions."

"Many of your people will be dead too if you ride through us, we will not die easily. So I ask why take something by force when it is offered as a gift."

Eochaid was stunned for a moment, and then he was intrigued. "What are you saying?"

"You and I can talk in the guard house, not in the open." With that Quintus simply turned and walked over to the guard house alone and opened the door. Turning to Eochaid he motioned for him to enter and waited.

Eochaid spoke quietly to two of the men nearest him then dismounted and followed Quintus.

Inside there was a table and five and one chairs but only Quintus and Eochaid entered and sat, either side of the table. Arberth and I entered as well though unseen.

In front of Quintus was a parchment with his seal on it.

"You probably know already that the Empire is overstretched." Began Quintus. "So we are withdrawing from this region. If we just left there would be chaos, we need someone to take over to govern this area. For instance you came with force to take the land, you were obviously intending to rule here."

Eochaid was silent.

"Can you read Eochaid?" Quintus went on. "It is in Latin because for us it is a legal document, but I can translate for you."

"I have made it my purpose to learn to read Latin. I can read."

Quintus turned the parchment towards him to read. Arberth and I read it and looked at each other.

'These humans never cease to surprise me.' He said.

'Yes, and I don't suppose any of the local people are going to be too happy.'

'They adapt.'

'That's true.'

Eochaid finished reading and sat silent for a while. Then he looked directly at Quintus.

"I am a warrior, not an administrator."

"No? So what were you going to do once you had driven us back? There would be opposition, you would have to fight all the people who live here, this way you simply take over with Roman authority. People will assume you could call on Roman military support if necessary, and to a limited extent that would be true because we are not going completely yet, will maintain a small garrison at Mordunum for a while."

Slowly Eochaid thought this through, he hadn't actually thought what would happen once he had driven the Romans out, he hadn't thought that the local people would be as much against him as the Romans. But with the Roman authority they would be less likely to move against him.

"This way much of the organisation for the area is already in place, you only have to take the lead and this document is your authority." Titus went on. "If you had got this by conquest there would have been no structure and there would be a lot of fighting between rival groups."

He remained silent.

"The title 'Protector' will give you our authority and people and as I said will assume our military support as well."

"I am a warrior, I am not used to fine palaces and I need to be among my men."

"We have already set up local people as regional governors throughout the province, they will be answerable to you. The administrative staff are in Mordunum but you do not need to live there, you can set up camp in the garrison in the next valley if you wish."

"Or here?"

"Or here. This is only a guard house but we can build a small fort for you."

What Eochaid did next surprised both Arberth and myself, he turned towards us. Because of his willingness to believe in our existence he had obviously been aware of our presence.

"I need to ask the gods." He said.

We knew he had enough belief in us for us to appear in physical form and from the way he reached out to us he clearly wanted us to so we did. Our surprise was nothing compared to the shock Quintius experienced.

"I do not know your names but I am glad you are here to witness this."

"I am Arberth." Said Arberth still not quite used to the name. "I am guardian of the land to the west."

"And I am Pwll'euad. Guardian of the valley to the east."

He stood and bowed to us. "Is this a good deal?"

"I don't know about Pwll'euad, I like a bit of fighting and bloodshed and a lot of burning, however it is a good deal. And it will probably save many of the people who live in my land." Said Arberth with a wicked glint in his eye as if he would be quite happy to set fire to the guardhouse.

"It is a peaceful way, whether it is a good deal will depend on you Eochaid and your dealings with the people as Protector. I see in you a wise and honest man who cares for people and I believe you could make it work." I said. "But why summon us? We are only servants of The Maker Of All Things."

"And if I do need your military help will I get that too?" Eochaid asked Quintus.

Quintius gazed open mouthed at us and didn't take his eyes off us. "Yes, of course, what little we can spare."

Eochaid sat back down and took the stylus from a stunned Quintus. Read over the parchment again and signed it.

"I hold you to your word Quintus, and what is more you now know there are other forces here you didn't know about, powerful forces, they are witnesses to this and you do not dare go back on this deal. You had better sign this now."

Glancing down briefly to sign he looked back at us.

Chapter 11

Castell Dwyrain

Eochaid Allmuir (Eochaid over the sea) and his men camped there while the Roman engineers and local labourers built a fortress similar to their outpost, Quintus arranged for food to be brought to them during the construction. A proclamation is made in every town and village in the west that Eochaid would be governor of. Eochaid watched the progress eagerly, if he had any doubts he didn't show. The fortress was just on Arberth's land so I generally left him to watch over things. However, Eochaid always wanted to consult both of us and Arberth was willing for this for a while.

In no time the fortress was built and the regional governors were commanded to come to Eochaid's official swearing in, he also wanted us there so it could be seen that not only did he have the authority of Rome but the blessing of the local gods as well.

For a few mornings while the preparations for the swearing in took place he stood silently at dawn and as the sun rose he called both our names. He was careful not to demand but because he was so persistent it was hard to see it any other way.

Arberth and I agreed not to attend, we are not answerable to him and we did not want to get involved in human politics, besides which although we saw it as a reasonable solution not a perfect one, it would maintain peace in our lands but they were being overrun by invaders again and we knew our people would not be happy, we could not condone this and certainly not give our blessing. Eochaid was very annoyed but there was nothing he could do.

Quintus swore him in with great ceremony and I felt he was relieved that we weren't there, he still couldn't get used to the idea that we existed and tried to blot us out of his memory. The fortress was named Castell Dwyrain (East Castle) because from Eochaid's perspective it was in the east. Every day he held court, sometimes here and sometimes in Mordunum, and I don't think anyone noticed Quintus and his men pack up and leave. Eochaid was actually a good leader and was used to command, and I suspect he did have some sort of administrative position in his homeland, and his skills he easily adapted to the running of the Roman administration he took over. He was also very wise and tended to judge according to the laws he had brought from his own land rather than Roman laws, but he was Governor and Protector and he could do as he chose.

The world had changed again and even without the Roman presence it was still a Roman world with its administrative structure, its taxes, its strict hierarchy and more and more square houses. Also much of the official business was carried out in Latin while Eochaid had to learn the local Celtic in order to talk to the local people.

Eochaid was so busy even he forgot about us and I settled back into the land and watched the seasons come and go. The people of the valley continued to do well and trade was good. The unattended outpost in my valley was taken apart by local farmers because of the quantity of good wood useful for their own building projects and soon there was only a mound.

I have often noticed that it didn't matter who was in charge, as long as everyone was left to carry on with their lives, without too much interference they simply got on with things as normal. Most people were unaffected by the Romans and were now unaffected by Eochaid. Of course there were always a vocal minority who stirred up a certain amount of resentment but most people were content to live in peace.

Eochaid married Liliwen who was descended from Ban though no one now remembered him and had forgotten why Petreban was called that. However being a local woman from what would have been the ruling family it was generally a popular move and I suspect it was a political marriage rather than for love. The wedding took place in a small chapel that had been built near Castell Dwyran on the border between Arberth and myself and was conducted by Brynmor, Bishop of Demed.

Brynmor was a humble, spiritual man. He spent his time walking over his diocese, encouraging his priests and visiting the sick. It was just fortunate that Liliwen had been to see Deri up in his stone hut to ask him to conduct the wedding when Brynmor turned up because Deri was more than happy to let the Bishop do the service. For Deri did not want to be involved with the Erin intruders and was quietly opposed to the marriage.

Brynmor on the other hand saw the wisdom of the marriage, as Bishop he understood the politics and had always to balance that with his care for people. He saw it as a peaceful way forward and a means of bringing unity back.

So when Corath was born the people began to feel they had their land and their lives back after so long under Roman domination. The Roman influence would be there in the valley for a long time still but the people now living knew of nothing else, there would be no way back to things as they were, time only flows one way. Corath was a good leader as was his son, Aed Brosc and his son, Trestin and his son, Alchol.

For the most part life went on much as it had before the Romans came after all it is the ordinary people who keep things going, they tend the land and the animals, they make, they trade. So there was peace and stability. They even told stories about me even though the religion was now Christian and the festivals held in the church dedicated to Mary and the other churches that were being built in the valley were the Christian festivals even if they did coincide with the older festivals, which was not by chance. So I simply became a legend and I was content.

Chapter 12

Rival Brothers

Alcol and his wife Anwen had two boys who they named Votepor and Conor. Votepor was the elder and immensely popular. He often came down to the church dedicated to Mary in the quiet of the early morning and would stand in the space outside to watch the sun come up. Not only did he care deeply for the people but he loved the natural world and felt a spirituality in it. He had sensed a difference in spirit between Arberth and myself and felt more at one with the peace in my valley. He was eager to listen to the stories that had been passed down, fragmentary and at times embellished as they were.

It was at the spring equinox as the sun rose that he realised the alignment of the bank round the church and he reached out to me with such urgency that I had to appear.

"It is true." He said rather surprised and a bit awed.

"Yes, it is true. You wished to see me?"

He was silent for a while so I took the opportunity to gaze about me at the valley, very little had changed outwardly. Votepor was a handsome youth, dark hair and eyes, very slight in stature.

"Well, I suppose I did. But really I only wanted to know if the old tales were true. I insist I am a Christian but I couldn't help wondering about you. I was sure I could feel something special about this valley, the peace and beauty. You are Pwll'euad?"

"And you are Votepor."

"You are a wise spirit, as well as beautiful and peaceful, I understand."

"I wouldn't say wise," Smiling at some of the things I have done which were not particularly wise. "I have seen a lot of things and I have not always been particularly peaceful."

"And you can see into the future."

"I cannot see into the future but I can see the present clearly."

"Can you tell me if I will make a good king?"

"King? That is one thing I didn't know, when did your family take on that title?"

"We were given the title by Rome."

"You were given the title Protector by Rome. But that doesn't matter. You want to know if you will make a good ruler. Yes, I can tell you that much for already you understand the people and they love you. But be careful of your brother."

"Oh, why?"

"Rivalry and jealousy I have seen too many times. He will stop at nothing so be aware."

"You surprise me, we are very close. Or I thought we were." He thought for a moment. "Are you sure about this?"

"I trust my experiences of humans. In nearly all cases there is not a problem between brothers, a little rivalry is not always bad. But when power is involved it is a different thing. And he sees the love people have for you which they do not have for him."

"I am still not sure you are right. However you will watch out for me?"

"I will do what I can but I cannot interfere, though that has never stopped me in the past. I cannot see the future so I cannot promise anything. Besides, this is your time and not mine, so you will excuse me, I interfere too much, I shouldn't have come."

And I was gone.

The seasons came and went and when his father died Votepor did indeed make a good ruler. He was organised and very fair and he opened up the chapel at Castell Dwyrain for the people of the area to come together for worship.

He often rode down to St. Mary's and stood in the enclosure and watch the sun come up. He constantly sought me, quietly calling my name. So eventually I relented.

"You shouldn't be looking for me." I said quietly behind him.

He turned. "I need your advice."

"No, you don't, you are a good ruler."

"You have been here a long time, you have seen many people come and go, you understand the people. This feels like a peaceful valley but I know it is not. There are factions, there is resentment between people, how do I keep peace with everyone?"

"Humans don't change, I have in the past tried to help with peace but too often there are people who do not want it. You are a complicated race. But what can I say, my kind are not always peaceful. I have no advice to give you except in your dealings with people, in your judgements of disputes, do not show favouritism."

He was silent for some time, deep in thought. "Can you tell me something of the people who lived here from long ago."

Sometimes the memories of those people still affect me deeply, with my kind a memory is like being there still and I still feel the loss of those I came very close to.

He must have read my pain in my face for he said. "I can see there is a lot of sadness, if you would rather not I will understand."

I sighed. "The first man I met gave me my name because he saw the moon reflected in the lake that was here ..." And from Ban onwards I told him of the many comings of people who settled in the valley and all the changes they brought. How the people were very resilient and how they would accept people from outside if they were willing to fit in with the local people.

I liked Votepor but I didn't think of him as a friend. In a way my reason for talking to him was a little selfish, a chance to take on human form for a while and to hear from him something of the world. The world had changed so much that I didn't want to get so involved with again. Still, I watched out for Votipor.

I also watched Conor as much as I could. He had gathered a large following from all over the region who gathered in the village of Arberth so I had no idea what he was planning. My cousin wasn't particularly interested so I had no news from him. I warned Votepor but as the brothers had little to do with each other he wasn't very concerned.

Although this part of the world was generally unaffected by the latest invasion from the mainland boats had made it round to the western coast and had set up a camp. Votepor went with a small force to face them. But he was a man of peace and as I couldn't be there I didn't know what happened. He was brought back critically injured and even I could do nothing to help. He died at Castell Dwyran and the people mourned.

It was significant that when his brother took on the name Vortepor and was declared King he also went to the invaders and I heard that he granted them the land which they named Angl. Of course no one believed I existed so I had to let things take their course.

Vortepor was after all the rightful successor and it was some time before he showed his true self. He built his palace at Arberth and from there ruled and he quickly became known as a tyrant and subjugated the people.

The people of my valley and many from further afield continued to mourn Votepor and they raised up a memorial stone to him at Castell Dwyran so although he had no heir himself they wanted him to be remembered.

The seasons came and went and the people rejoiced when Vortepor died a horrible death and his son Congar took his place. Congar was only young and many of Votepor's advisors were able to help him.

CHAPTER 13

Saint Canna

A woman came to Sarnlas from the north in the early hours of the autumn equinox when the mist still lay in the valley and the sky above was blue and cloudless, the air still. She stood for some time looking across the valley and breathed the air deeply. I could sense a deep peace within her, a peace that comes with a sure faith, she was very open and I could sense she had travelled much and done much in the cause of The Son Of The Maker Of All Things who she seemed to know very well. What surprised me was that she was reaching out to me even though she can have known nothing about me.

"I know there is a peaceful spirit in this valley and I know you are not an angel."

'Oh Maker Of All Things, should I appear?' I felt so close to her I so wanted to meet her in person.

"Do not worry, you will not confuse my beliefs, for you are a creature of the Most High and a servant as I am."

I knew I liked her and yearned to have a human friend again after so much time, even if for a fleeting moment.

"In the Name of Jesus, Son of God, I ask your name."

"Pwll'euad." It just slipped out as I found myself standing before a middle aged woman with greying hair a plump friendly face and penetrating blue eyes. She was a little shorter than me and dressed simply is a coarse russet coloured dress over a linen blouse. Very rarely I have met someone who has a glow about them as if lit from an inner light, this was one such person, there was a radiance about her face that came from her love of the Son Of The Maker Of All Things.

"And I am Canna, daughter of Tudur, widow of Saint Sadwrn and sister in law of Saint Illtyd."

"I am sorry." I said, bowing my head. "I shouldn't be here."

"Maybe not, but please, do not bow your head you and I are both servants. But why Pwll'euad, where is the pool?"

"There was a lake a long time ago."

"What happened to the lake?"

Suddenly I was filled with a flood of sadness as I remembered Little Rainbow. Sometimes it is hard to take on human form because it is not my natural state and am not used to the feelings that can overwhelm me when I do.

I found myself held tight in Canna's embrace. It was a strange feeling, I have been close to Silverwheel but this was different, it was as if I was a child being comforted by her mother, there was such a love emanating from Canna that I have never known in a human.

"I'm sorry." She whispered. "I will not ask again."

She released me and gave me space to compose myself.

"I know you are not human even in this form but you obviously feel as we do. You may be an ancient spirit but really you are a child as a human, you still do not understand your feelings in this form." She said at last. "But our Lord was totally human and I often wonder while feeling all that we do what he must have learnt as God from that even though God is unchanging."

"You and I are bound in time, he is not." I said. "From his perspective the time he spent in human form has always been part of him."

She smiled as if something that had worried her for a long time no longer did.

"I see you understand time." She said. "But you would, you have seen so much of it."

"No, I don't understand time at all."

"Then it is your not understanding of time that helps understand God being outside of time."

I didn't understand that statement either and I must have looked confused. She burst out laughing and her laugh was such that I couldn't help but laugh with her. It struck me that I rarely laugh, the last time was a long time ago with a little girl. And although Canna was a mature woman she made me feel young again.

"Who is the local priest and who is the local ruler?" She asked when we stopped laughing.

"Ioraeth is the priest, when he is not with his colleagues in Mordunum he is in a small stone hut across there, in fact he is there now." I pointed across the valley to the hill where the hut was. "Congar calls himself king and he has a palace in Arberth village over that way and is often in Mordunum holding court." And I pointed to the west. "You are fortunate for at the moment he is on the way back to Arberth and has gone to see Ioraeth while he is passing through, so you will find them both there."

"Good. Could you do me a favour?"

"If it won't get me into trouble with The Maker Of All Things."

"Well, it is two favours actually. You are the valley and therefore I assume that through the valley you can summon everyone here."

"I can do that, I don't suppose he will mind."

"As for the second favour, when they are here and I give the word can you make this staff burst into leaf?" And she lifted up the staff she had been leaning on.

"And if he doesn't approve?"

"He will have me to answer to."

"I don't know." I said doubtfully. "Isn't it being deceptive? You are supposed to be a holy woman sent by The Maker Of All Things, you are supposed to be the one to perform miracles."

"Perspective again. All of nature is a miracle from the human perspective. Nature is who you are. Every miracle I have ever heard of is actually natural but is an unusual way."

I tried to reach out to The Maker Of All Things and it was as if valley all round laughed, people don't think of Him laughing but he does, and he cries too.

This was all the answer I was going to get so I dug my toes into the soil where I stood and commanded all who were in the valley to gather in the area below where we were, where the Roman road passed through. Everyone felt the compulsion without understanding why and although some would have resisted they followed those who felt the impulse or simply came out of curiosity. It took some time but they all came, a vast number filling the valley, how different from the last time I did this and they had filled the sanctuary where the small Church to Mary now stood. I let go of my physical presence and waited with Canna in spirit form only, to appear to so many would definitely be interfering.

"Congar and Ioraeth." She called out. "Please come up here and stand with me."

They climbed up to where she was, looking perplexed, they didn't know what just happened.

"Why are we here?" Asked Congar. "Did you somehow compel us?"

"She didn't." Said Ioraeth and he glanced to where I stood invisibly or so I thought.

Congar looked somewhat perplexed at Ioraeth and then at Canna.

"You are here and that is what matters." Canna said and she raised her staff, she nodded in my direction and it budded into leaf and for effect I made a blossom sprout on the tip.

Ioraeth looked in my direction and smiled.

"I come with the authority of Sadwrn and Illtyd. I have come to set up a church here."

Then I was gone. What Canna had to say was between her and the people of the valley.

They obviously believed, or at least many of them did, because they soon got to work and set up a church on the site. Over the years that followed many pilgrims stopped off there on their way to St. David's Cathedral using the Roman road as far as it went.

Canna rose early every morning and sat on a bank overlooking the Roman Road. She wanted me to sit with her so I did with gladness, she was the friend I had craved for a long time. She did not expect me to be anything other than myself, she understood my position in the order of spirits, my existence didn't interfere with here deep, deep faith. I was comfortable with her and she with me.

"Canna, you are a follower of the Son and you know him well, so I have to ask why do you wish to talk to me?"

"I like you, I hope we are friends as much as is possible."

Friends, we were, but I have lost so many and Canna would not live for ever either, but friends we could be even if the time was short.

"You are a good guardian of the valley." She said.

"But I have interfered too often with the people of the valley. I am sure The Maker Of All Things must disapprove at times, maybe get a bit annoyed with me."

"That is what guardians do. And I can tell you this, God has never disapproved of you, he has been rather amused at times, he trusts you more than you can know."

"It has not always been for the good, and there has still been fighting and bitterness. I am sure there are times when I have been wrong."

"And yet you have kept a peace here no matter what the people have done. The valley has that sense of peace and it surely affects people who live here. I know there are people within the valley who will never know peace in their hearts but that is not your fault, sadly it is human nature. As for being wrong at times, there often is no right or wrong, you and I both live in time and cannot predict the future, we do our best with what we know now, in that we are the same, I have been wrong too."

I didn't reply to this, I wasn't sure that I was that peaceful at times, in fact I knew I wasn't and I couldn't imagine Canna ever being wrong.

"I cannot stay here for long. There is much work to do elsewhere." She said after a while. "I find peace sitting and talking with you, when I do move on I may not find such peace. Let us be friends for a while so I can store up these memories for where Jesus sends me next."

Days later we sat silently when suddenly she turned to me.

"I know you are not human but you do have human feelings and emotions." She said.

"In this form I do."

"And in spirit?"

"Not as intense but over the years I have come to separate the two less. Until I took on human form I had never known feelings, but now the feelings spill into my spirit."

"You have had great sadness, and because you are ageless you have suffered loss over and over again."

"It is the way of things."

"So, who do you talk to about it?"

"Selene, she may not be my mother in the sense you would understand but she has always been a mother to me. We talk a lot."

She reflected for a moment before she went on. "Would it help to talk to me? I, at least, am human all the time and am quite used to feelings and emotions."

I thought it might help and here was a woman of experience who I could trust but I hesitated.

"I am curious though." She said looking out across the valley. "You are the valley, or the valley's guardian, you can take on human form with all the feeling that go with it, could you become totally human if you chose? And what would happen to the valley if you did."

I wasn't sure if this was just curiosity or had she sensed something in me that was at the heart of my deepest sadness and cruellest hurt. I drew my knees close and said nothing, I could not trust my voice at that moment.

"Oh." She said. "I am sorry, I seem to have hit on a deep hurt or loss and I apologise, I will ask no more questions."

"A long time ago." I began, hesitantly and sighed, I let go of my knees and gazed out across the valley. "A long time ago there was a lake here, the first settler saw the moon reflected on the surface of the lake and absently gave me my name."

I told her about Little Rainbow, how she became human and because she was the waterfall there could be no waterfall and the lake broke through and flowed away, how she lived a very long time before she died.

"I believe The Maker Of All Things took her to the Otherworld, I hope I am right. What do you think?"

"I am sure he did. What happens to your people otherwise?"

"If we don't go on we simply get forgotten and fall asleep. I don't know what then, perhaps we are not supposed to know."

"The Almighty wastes nothing, there has to be a place for you. But that is not all is it, or would you rather not say."

I told her how I was taken in by Llewellyn and thought I loved him, I almost became fully human for him but found out about him in time, and that hurt me deeply. That was my one choice and I chose not to become human.

"You chose well, Pwll'euad. There are men who are worthy and it is not always easy to discover them. Llewellyn is a waste of your emotions and feelings, you are a good and kind spirit and this valley would be a dark place without you."

I nodded.

"But Little Rainbow almost broke your heart and you haven't got over that. Firstly because she chose to be human and you felt responsible, you are still not sure if it was you who broke through the gap and emptied the lake, I can assure you it was not you. Secondly as you watched over her and she slowly aged and eventually died and you had to let her go, in fact you haven't let her go and you need to. You believe she was accepted into the Otherworld, your description of her passing shows she did, but still you lost her and you are afraid possibly for ever because you don't know God's ultimate plan for you."

I just sat quietly with my thoughts. She was right, I didn't know how to let go.

"If it helps I was told to come here." She said. "I was told someone needed me, someone who will be invaluable in the future but needed to face her past first. I thought it was a person and I have been looking for her all the time I have been here, but now I know it was you, I was sent to help you."

I looked at her but I still couldn't speak.

"I will stay a while longer but I feel I have done what I was sent here for. The rest is up to you."

Canna stayed for some time but she got restless, she set her sights on a town to the East. Before she left she came to the small church by the river in the early morning, wishing to see me.

"Pwll'euad." She said as I stood beside her and watched the sun come up. "Thank you for your help, Ioraeth is quite capable of looking after things while I have other work to do."

"I'm glad to have spent some time with you."

"Will you miss me?"

"I miss a lot of people for such is the difference between my kind and yours. Yet I will miss you more than anyone."

"You can probably talk to Ioraeth."

"It is time I kept out of things. Christianity is the main faith now and it is time for humanity to make their own way. Many of my kind have faded long ago and I don't know why I hang on. But where are you going?"

"I am going to Llandaff, perhaps I will set up a church near there for I feel it will be an important centre in the future. Many of our pilgrims pass through there and I hear encouraging stories."

"Taff is generally a good spirit but he does tend to be a bit full of his own importance, I shouldn't say this but I don't suppose you will find peace with him."

"I will bear that in mind."

We embraced for the last time and she strode off into the East. I let go of my physical presence content to settle into the quiet of the valley and the passing of the seasons.

Chapter 14

The Exorcism

Bishop Lucius first appeared striding along the road in a heavy cloak embroidered with Christian symbols, a wooden staff in his hand representing a shepherds crook. He paused at the junction with the by-road that used to lead to the roman garrison and looked about for a moment. Pentreban had now become the main settlement, many of the houses built in the square Roman style. Sarnlas had simply become an agricultural settlement around the small church dedicated to Saint Canna.

He marched into Pentreban and made himself known.

"I am Bishop Lucius and I come from Canterbury with good news. The Pope himself has decreed that you no longer follow the worship of many gods but the one true God and his Son Jesus Christ. I have come also to stamp out the pagan practices that many of you still hold on to."

The people had gathered round him, unsure what to make of it all.

"Show me your temple and I will cast out all evil from it that it may be a church to the Most High."

"There is no temple but there are many churches." Said a man in a simple priests robe.

"And you are?"

"Elgan. We are a Christian community. We have no pagan practices here."

Lucius looked about him first at the gathered people, then the hills beyond.

"This is a valley and a river runs through it. You have an ancient god, I know it. Everywhere has an ancient god. Show me where his temple is."

"There is no temple."

"Is there a church by a river here? That is where the temple would be."

"That is St. Mary's church, it has been a church back as far as Christianity first came here."

"Then take me there, I expect it was built on a pagan site and needs to be cleansed." He demanded.

"As you wish, but there is nothing evil there." Said Elgan shrugging. "Follow me."

St Mary's church was still a simple wooden building where the people of the village would gather whenever Elgan was there, for he travelled far and wide from church to church, from community to community. Several of the villagers followed, eager to find out what this was all about.

"Good, this is the place, I know it." Said Lucius. "You may go."

"If you need me I am going to St. Canna's next, then St Teilo's in Castell Dwyran. I won't be back this way for some time but send someone for me if you do need me."

"I shall not need you, you may go about your work."

Staff in hand, Elgan said his goodbyes to many of the gathered people, walked back through Pentreban and up to Sarnlas.

Lucius looked around at the gathered people. "It will not be safe for you here for I will be contending against great evil, you had all better go back to whatever it was you were doing."

Then he entered the enclosure and picked a position in the centre. "By the blood of Jesus Christ I cleanse this place." He cried out.

Lucius somehow compelled me to be there before him though he did not have enough belief for me to appear in physical form. We were in the sacred space and he was claiming it as his.

"Evil Spirit I command you to name yourself." He called out, raising his arms, making the sign of the cross with his right hand.

He bent down and picked up a bowl of water with his left hand and dipping the first two fingers of his right hand began to sprinkle the water in my direction and then all around himself, then back to my direction again.

"In the name of Jesus Christ and the power of his shed blood I sanctify this place and I command you to reveal yourself."

He could not see me but he must have been able to sense my presence.

"By the authority of God's Holy Church I claim this land for his glory, I demand you reveal yourself and be cast down into the depths of hell, to eternal fire and damnation."

How could he claim the land? It belonged to The Maker Of All Things anyway and he had placed me here as guardian, he had never asked me to leave so by what authority did this man have? I saw in this the Roman influence trying to exert itself again.

He was getting quite heated and red in the face. He held his crook before him as if it was some sort of magical talisman.

"Child of Satan I command you, name your name. By the power of Almighty God, by the shed blood of Jesus Christ, by the authority of the holy church, I command you to name your name."

"Moonpool."

The voice came from behind me but it was not directed at Lucius nor could he hear it, it was directed solely at me.

I turned. I knew The Son Of The Maker Of All Things. I knelt to him.

"Moonpool, stand on your feet."

I stood and try as I might not to look directly at him he drew my gaze to himself, I could hear Lucius ranting behind me but as if from a vast distance, for all my world at that moment was the Son.

He smiled and nodded towards Lucius, "He assumes too much, he does not speak for me at all, this is a test of his power alone. You are not evil either, you are nature, my Father created you good and you have always chosen the good."

I spoke hesitantly. "He compelled me to be here."

"He has a partial belief in spirits. You notice he didn't have enough faith for you to physically appear."

"What should I do? He'll keep on until he learns my name."

"The name Ban gave you, but who were you before?"

"I had no name."

"Then if you have no name yourself except what a man gave you then you cannot reveal it. He wastes his breath and it is his to waste. He is human and will soon wear himself out. You can stay and watch or go, the choice is yours."

"Should I respond to him at all?"

"No, to do so will confirm his suspicions. Leave him with his doubts. But if it bothers you by my authority take on human form outside the sanctuary and wait for him to come to you, he will not expect the evil spirit there and will think you are human. Besides you do not look like the sort of evil spirit he would be expecting." And he smiled a radiant and, if I may say so, a mischievous smile.

And he was gone, or as much gone as the omnipresent Son Of The Maker Of All Things can be.

I turned back to Lucius who was getting redder and redder in the face, sweating profusely and shouting what sounded to me now like gibberish.

I may have mentioned before that the weather spirits can be rather devious, dark clouds rolled in and the rain began to pelt down. The people who had stayed, despite his warning, deserted Lucius and ran for cover, as far as they were concerned the contest was over and Lucius was either deranged or had lost the battle.

Lucius fell to the ground in despair. I did feel a little sorry for him for I have seen what humiliation does to humans. But this was not my doing. I was not going to interfere with his life. He must face the consequences of his own choice.

He got up and walked away, his head bowed and his feet dragging. The rain eased and the clouds began to roll away. So I took on human form as The Son suggested and by his authority and I met Lucius just outside the sanctuary.

"Oh dear." I said brightly. "You do look absolutely worn out, I do feel sorry for you, can I help?" I was not gloating. All I wanted to do was to help if I could.

He looked up at me with despair in his eyes.

"Have you been in a fight or something?" I asked.

"Not a fight as you would understand it." His voice was hoarse and weak.

"I think I do. I have a message from The Son Of The Maker Of All Things."

"You? And who are you?"

"My name is Pwll'euad. I live in this valley." In a strange way I felt relieved by telling him.

"And how do you have a message from the Son?"

"How is not important. Just this. You have been shouting in his sanctuary where there is no need. The battle has already been won a long time ago. Seek him only and you will find peace."

He looked back at the sanctuary and I took the opportunity to be gone.

When he turned to look at me again and saw nothing he began to wonder, but at least he was calmer as if a weight had been lifted from him.

He knelt down on the wet ground and clasped his hands together. A ray of sun broke through the clouds onto him. His prayer was between him and The Maker Of All Things so I left.

He entered the village humble and soaked to the skin. The people were good and a family welcomed him in, sat him before a fire, dried his clothes while he huddled in a blanket and gave him some broth to warm him up.

I knew Elwyn, the father, very well. He was directly descended from Ban and I have often found that good blood flows though families as does bad. He knew about me since old legends are remembered through families for many generations. In the quiet of his mind he reached out to me briefly to ask if I was alright.

Because of his belief I was able to take on human form, which I did, but outside. Then I knocked on the door.

"Come in." Called Elwyn.

"Pwll'euad." Elwyn greeted me as I entered. "How are you, I was very concerned."

He had been a witness to Lucius' attempt to drive me out and wondered if it had affected me in any way.

"I have been talking to the Son Of The Maker Of All Things and I came to see how Lucius was, I was worried after he got so worked up at the church."

Elwyn smiled.

Lucius looked up at me from his hunched up position under the blanket, a puzzled look on his face.

Elwyn saw the puzzled expression.

"Oh, Pwll'euad is a friend of the family." He said. "She has helped my family countless times."

Lucius looked me up and down, my dress must have seemed very strange, and he stared at my bare feet.

"I want to thank you for what you said down at the church." He said. "But how have you been talking to the Son? And how come you are dry? And why do you refer to God as The Maker Of All Things?"

I could sense that he had an odd feeling about me, he had sensed my presence before but hadn't quite made the connection.

"So, how are you feeling now? Will you be staying long?" I asked without answering any of his questions.

"I don't know what I should be doing now, I was so sure of my mission before, I think I need to return and spend time in prayer, I need to find myself again."

"I will leave Elwyn to look after you then, he is a good man and you can learn a lot from him."

"I hope you will call again." Said Elwyn. "There is much I would like to talk to you about."

"I cannot promise." There probably would be no harm, but I felt I was treading a fine line.

I left through the door before I was gone.

Lucius stayed a few days, Elgan returned and in his simple way was able to help Lucius whose faith had been sorely tested. But Elgan's deep faith encouraged and restored Lucius' until he was ready to move on, but no more driving out demons unless it was necessary. However I did wonder how many he had driven out on his way here, I am sure there are some of my kind who could do with a good talking to.

Chapter 15

Hunting Party

Many seasons came and went. Fewer pilgrims passed along the old Roman Road as time passed without the Son returning and people began to drift away from Christianity. Locally people began to get disillusioned because a Roman hierarchy had been imposed on the church and the higher ranking clergy had become distant and the church wasn't so community based. St. Mary's fell into disuse, those who still believed went to St. Canna's where it was believed wrongly that there was a holy well. Further afield within my valley there were churches dedicated to St. Brynach further up the Gronw and St. David on the Marlais in the Velfrey area. Though neither saint had ever been near here.

I must have been elsewhere, floating on the wind or resting in the ground, when a hunting party arrived on horseback at the old sanctuary where St. Mary's was little more than a pile of rotten timbers, and I suppose it was their arrival at this place that drew my attention. Llywarch, the king, was there with some of his men and a group from away.

"Cadell." Llywarch addressed the man who was the head of the visitors. "How do you like this spot?"

Cadell looked round at the valley approvingly. He looked down at the bank that enclosed the area.

"This is an ancient site." He remarked. "I expect there is an old god associated with it."

"Maybe. No one remembers now. There was a little church here a long time ago, the area isn't used now. I thought this would be a good place to set up a hunting lodge, for although it is by the river it never floods and any supplies we need we can bring up the river."

"Is the hunting good here? There seems to be a lot of farm land."

"This is a good river for trout and there is plenty of woodland in the hills where there is game. Besides, it is the festivities after the hunt that are just as important as the hunt itself, and we can set up a sizeable camp on the flat land here."

"Ah, and this will give us the chance to talk and forge alliances."

"Indeed."

They shared knowing looks.

A wooden hunting lodge was soon built within the enclosure and a larger party arrived. Temporary huts and stalls were set up in the flat plane behind reminiscent of the gatherings I had seen when the sanctuary was used regularly.

Cadell had many of his important people with him as well as his son Hywell. Hywell was a tall young man, very open so I could have read his thought had I wished, a very wise and astute man for one so young.

Llywarch had no son but he had a daughter Elen. Elen was still young enough to believe in things that older people learned to dismiss, I could speak to her in the transition from sleep to full wakefulness but I held back. I didn't want to interfere. I understood what it was that Llywarch and Cadell planned. The uniting of the large northern kingdom and the kingdom of Demed would give the two families a greater say in the changing world, a voice in the royal court to the East.

That night I watched the hunting party as they gathered round a fire by the river and noticed that Cadell drank freely of the wine that Llywarch provided but Llywarch drank sparingly. So I waited. Elen was interested in old stories and legends, and had even heard something of me. Her belief was strong enough for me to take on physical form which I did while keeping out of sight, this was easy enough as it was dark and the moon was a new moon. I was intrigued and it is easier to physically hear people talking, I hoped I would overhear something usefull. Llywarch and a few of his men were the only ones still awake.

"Are you sure about this Mabon?" Llywarch asked one of the younger men.

"Certain. With this you will triumph over all others, you will be all powerful."

"And there is one here?"

"In the woods up there. My source said he saw it with his own eyes, even if it was only fleetingly." He pointed in a general way to the south west.

"And only a maiden can do this?"

"So I understand. But we have to be ready."

"Tomorrow then, and then I no longer need come begging to Cadell for an alliance." He leaned back, satisfied. "The power will be mine."

There always seems to be some intrigue going on among the humans, some secret only a few know, or think they do for nothing is ever as secret as those keeping it know. But this was probably not my business, these were all outsiders. Yet, if it would affect the valley it would be worth keeping a watch, especially as it seemed to involve Elen who was innocent of whatever it was they were planning. And what did they think was in the woods?

The next day Llwarch sent Elen alone up into the hills to the west, up into the woods. I was worried for her, I wasn't sure what the plan was but I was sure it wasn't good. How could he send his young daughter alone up into the woods, he didn't know what dangers there might have been. As she went I waited for her just before she entered the woods.

"Hello Elen." I said brightly.

"Hello." She said. "Do you live around here? And how do you know me?"

"I am here." I said. "And I know you because you have been trying to find out about me. I am Pwll'euad."

"Pwll'euad, that is an unusual name, you are not the nature spirit I have stories of are you?" She was excited. "I have wanted to meet one of your kind for a long time."

"Since no one else believes in me then for them you are still alone. But I am rather concerned, you don't mind if I keep you company do you?"

"Oh, please do."

As we walked along I wondered if Elen knew what this was about.

"What are you supposed to do all on your own?"

"Find a glade in the woods, sit and sing and wait."
"Wait for what, or is it who?"

"A unicorn. Oh I do hope to see a unicorn."

"Oh, of course, a unicorn, that makes sense." So Llwarch was after a unicorn horn believing in the legends about drinking from the horn gave great power. No need for an alliance then.

"I know an ideal glade." I said. "Come, follow me."

We found the glade and she sat down on a fallen log and began to sing and wait. Of course no unicorn came.

In the distance a pack of baying hounds could be heard and they were coming closer. I placed a deep peace over the glade, so when they suddenly burst in upon us they stopped barking and running, with their tongues hanging out and their tails wagging they ambled over to Elen and lay down.

The peace, the warmth of the sun, the scents of tree and flower heavy in the air, the very atmosphere caused drowsiness.

When Llewarch and his men came riding into the glade they found all the dogs asleep. Elen had fallen asleep too. The horses stopped their gallop so suddenly the men almost fell off. Llewarch tried to urge his horse on but his horse started crazing instead.

"Do not force your horse Llewarch." I shouted as I grew to twice my size and extended my wings. "You intrude on sacred ground."

Llewarch fell off his horse badly and dislocated his shoulder.

"Take him back and do not come here again." I commanded his men as I picked him up and lay him across his horse.

The men cowered before me, I can be somewhat intimidating when I want. The horses all turned and trotted back the way they came, the riders had no control over them. The dogs woke up and padded after the horses.

I folded away my wings and returned to my normal size and waited for Elen to wake up.

She stretched herself and yawned and sat up. Blinking she looked about her then at me and smiled.

"Have I been asleep long?" She asked.

"I wouldn't know how long 'long' is."

"Did a unicorn come and I missed it?"

"No, no unicorn. You do realise unicorns are mythical."

"So are you."

I smiled.

CHAPTER 16

White House

The next day Llywarch seemed to age suddenly, although his shoulder was put back he wasn't able to use his right arm and he was in constant pain. The earth circled the sun only once and he died.

After the funeral at St Canna's and the embers of the pyre were fading and the ashes scattered to the wind Cadell stood with Elen looking down into the valley as the sun began to rise on a new day.

"Elen, you are Queen now." Said Cadell. "That is a heavy responsibility."

Perhaps it was too soon for him to mention this but I sensed a strength in Elen. She was brought up to know what her role would be, it is just that she didn't expect it so soon.

"I know my duty." She looked directly at Cadell who was surprised at her maturity. "There was to be an alliance, or there should have been but apparently my father had other plans which will never happen now. I know he was a scheming man and I was never really close to him. As for me, I believe in the alliance, in this changing world we need the strength of unity. Perhaps we can work on that."

Cadell took Elen under his protection as she was now Queen and because of her age she was glad of his support and advice. The earth circled the sun again and Hywel and Elen were married at Saint David's Cathedral by the Bishop, all the dignitaries were there. Elen even invited me, I asked permission from the nature spirit there and he granted it willingly, and I watched in spirit, only she knew I was there.

They travelled the length and breadth of the Kingdom, listened to the concerns of the nobility and the ordinary people alike. Hywel learned a great deal about the people and of the responsibility he would eventually have.

In due time Cadell himself died and Hywel became King of the United Kingdoms of the west.

Hywel proved a wise and popular king, a man who not only understood his own people but fully understood the politics of the age as well. He was willing to bow the knee to the English Kings and he travelled to Rome to meet with the Pope.

In Rome he was impressed by the architecture and decided to copy it on a smaller scale. So he brought white stone from the south west to build a larger and more impressive lodge. He had plans for his kingdom, and needed somewhere impressive to bring people together.

Elen often stood watching the builders and while they were occupied I stood quietly beside her.

"Monapool." She used my new Anglo-Saxon name.

I smiled.

"What are you smiling about?" She asked.

"Monapool, I have had a few names as the languages here have changed but it will take some getting used to, some still call me Pwll'euad."

"Hywel is a good man, you told me that once and you were right too."

"Hywel is a good and a wise man. Already they call him Hywel Dda."

I could see that although the marriage was not originally out of love but need Elen was deeply in love with Hywel now. I also knew that Hywel always was in love with Elen.

"Elen." I said after a while. "I am happy for you both, I see that you are both in love. This love has grown slowly."

Elen beamed brightly. Then she frowned a little.

"This place he is calling Ty Gwyn Ar Daf, and he will call the village over there by that name too. I hope Pentreban hasn't an important significance to you." She said.

I sighed. In human form I still feel deeply the loss of Ban for with us memory is an ever present reality.

"Ban was the first human I met." I said, but not with sadness. "He first named me in the language now forgotten. You have his blood in you."

"Then I'm sorry Hywel has renamed his village."

"All things human change."

"Hywel's white house, he is building it on a place that is special to you though."

"Yes, and therefore it will be special again. It is a thin place, we are close to the Otherworld here, I am sure that will help with Hywel's plan."

"You don't appear to Hywel."

"Hywel has no time for fantasies, he is a very practical and politically astute man."

Elen smiled.

And so it was a special place again. When the house was built Hywel summoned the lords and chieftains from all over his kingdom of Deheubarth to formally unite the kingdoms and to bring together a set of laws for the land.

Once again the field behind was covered with temporary dwellings for all the servants of the nobles and for those who provided provisions and entertainment. There were exotic foods from distant lands, musicians in groups playing music, jugglers and fire eaters. While Hywel held his meetings in the white house, which was indeed impressive, Elen and I walked through the camp.

"Do you eat?" She asked and she sampled some sugared dates from a distant land.

"I could but I never have."

"Did you want to try?" She offered me some.

"Ah, in human form there are many distractions to my kind and a good many have become human because of them and it never ends well."

She looked at me intently. "You are sad."

I looked up in the direction where Little Rainbow's waterfall was once. I sighed. "There is much sadness in this world I sometimes wonder why The Maker Of All Things made it so."

"You are spirit and are surely above such things."

"I am also nature and the whole of nature groans with humanity. We wish to help but humans want to go their own way. I am also sad because I have had many friends among your people and your lives are so short." Then I drew a deep breath and smiled. "But I am content as I am. The present is full of hope. Do you hear everyone from wherever they are call each other Cymraeg?"

"Yes, Hywel has already done so much good. I do hope this lasts."

"You are with child and that is always good for the future."

Elen would have dropped her dates if I hadn't caught them.

"You didn't know?"

"I wasn't sure." She put her hand to her belly and there was a light in her eyes. "But now I know for sure I will tell Hywel tonight. You will keep me and the child safe?"

"When you are here. But you have a large kingdom and my valley is only a small part of it."

We came to a tent of a fortune teller.

"Shall we go in?" Asked Elen. "Maybe she can tell me about my child."

"Why not, perhaps she can tell me something as well."

It was a dark tent with a dim, flickering lamp and the heavy smell of incense and spices.

"Welcome to Una's mystic tent." Said the old woman hunched up over a table with a bowl of water in the middle, a shawl over her head, and jangly bracelets on her wrists. "I see many things if you have the gold."

Elen placed two small gold coins on the table. "For me and my friend."

"Sit." Said Una indicating two chairs opposite her.

We sat.

"Your hand." Said the woman.

Elen reached out her hand to her, she took it and examined it for a while then let go. She waved her hands over the water and gazed into it.

"You are with child, you will have a daughter."

"Boy." I whispered.

"She will be a great lady." Una continued either not hearing me or ignoring what I said. "She will marry a man of noble birth." She waved her hands over the water. "I see clearer now. Your husband is a great man I see, and you will be wealthy. You will live a long and happy life and you will travel far and wide."

I could sense Elen was trying not to laugh.

"Now your hand." Una said to me.

I held out my hand and she held it for a while then let it go and waved her hands over the water.

"I cannot tell your future, you have a deep sadness in your past that you have not let go of. A death? Yes and no, I cannot tell. A daughter and yet not a daughter. Also I sense ..."

She lifted the shawl a little to look directly at me. Her piercing eyes looking deep into mine. Then she bowed her head.

"Does Elen know who you are?"

"Yes I do." Said Elen.

"I am honoured that both of you should come into my tent, the Queen and the Goddess."

"I am not a goddess." I said. "Just guardian of the valley."

She pushed the coins back to Elen. "Before you go Pwll'euad, can you bless me?"

I admit I was expecting something made up and was surprised that she was quite genuine, apart from getting the gender of the baby wrong.

"I see you are a true seer." I said as I put my hand on her head. "What blessing I can give I do, but your own insight is your best gift."

There were many laws to discuss from all over the kingdom, many old traditions and wise judgements, some written but most handed down by word of mouth, but Hywel was determined to leave nothing out and to give everyone a chance to speak. The sun passed from its highest and was approaching the equinox by the time Hywel had his book of laws and the scribes began to copy it. Standing on the bank where Ban's ashes had been he held the book aloft.

"Cymraeg!" He shouted in a voice that carried over the field and all faces turned to him. "Here are your laws, you are one people now with one law, one heart and one mind."

Everyone cheered.

Chapter 17

Hermit Sten

There are times I almost despair of humanity. The kingdom didn't stay united, for there was rivalry between his sons. There was fighting among his descendants. But it is not my place to recount events that had little bearing on the land. Rather I continued to care for the valley and the people in it.

A man came to the small stone hut to the south of the valley. He was one of the raiders from a distant land to the north who had settled in Arberth. He wore a coarse woollen robe with a leather belt. His hair and beard were a wild and unkempt reddish colour. His face was downcast and being an open person I could see he was riddled with guilt. He had come with a raiding party and had spilt innocent blood and now he had come across Christianity and felt he could never atone for what he had done. He had left his people and walked off into the countryside to find some sort of peace, to seek a place away from people where he could pray in isolation.

The stone hut was still standing though ivy had grown up over much of it. Sten set about removing the ivy without dislodging the stones. Then he cleared out the inside and made it somewhat habitable. He cut grasses and let them dry in the sun before spreading them on the floor of the hut. When all this was done he knelt down and prayed and wept until after the sun went down.

Even in an out of the way place like the stone hut the people of the valley knew he was there. There was much talk about him and people were wondering why he was there. He was reckoned by most to be a holy man and therefore he would have something wise to teach.

Eleri, a woman from the village of Ty Gwyn who had lost two children in childbirth was the first to summon up the courage to consult him. He saw her coming along the track that passed near the hut and thought only that she was passing so was surprised when she turned to approach. Although he had come here to be away from people, to pray and think in isolation he found he was lonely and it would be nice to talk to someone.

"Hello." He said not unkindly. "What brings you to my little Kiffig?"

"Kiffig?"

"Yes." Indicating the stone hut. "I know not what it is in your tongue."

"Nor do I really, Kiffig it is then. I need your help."

"I cannot help myself so I don't know how I can help you."

"You are a holy man, you talk to God up here all alone."

"I talk but I don't know if he hears and I am certainly not a holy man. But I don't mind talking for a while, what is your name?"

"Eleri. I have had two children lost at birth and I want to ask you is it because I have sinned?"

"God doesn't punish the innocent for our sin. It seems he doesn't punish the guilty either. I have been told that he is merciful and forgives sin which is harder for us to bear when we cannot forgive ourselves."

"I know I am not always a good person, I try to be better but it is very hard. Are you trying to say I cannot forgive myself for something and that is why I lost two babies?"

"You cannot possibly be as sinful as I am."

"But you are here, in this old hut that has been used by holy men before, you pray to God, you cannot be a sinful man."

"I pray to God to wash the blood from my hands and my heart."

Eleri looked at his hands, then looked into his eyes.

"You don't look like a sinful man, you look so kind and understanding, perhaps God has heard your prayers."

"You are kind. Besides to lose two babies is not a punishment, nor is it something you are bringing on yourself, but I don't suppose it will help you if I say it is simply part of nature and no one is to blame."

"So I must accept that losing my babies is not a punishment, but it hurts so very much."

"You are a good woman, I only wish I could help you."

In a strange way as they talked together they both helped each other. Since there were so many people in the valley now I was not able to keep up with everyone and I hadn't known about Eleri. I felt guilty that I hadn't been there for her. I thought back over all the births I had helped with, particularly Lia and Little Rainbow and the joy of a mother and therefore how much pain and sadness Eleri felt. I reached inside her and found her problem, a simple thing for me to put right.

Other people came to Sten at the Kiffig, he could not understand why, and each one found consolation from him and he in turn felt he was in some way making up for his earlier life. And when Eleri gave birth to a healthy strong boy she named him Sten. This was seen as a miracle and more and more people flocked to the Kiffig to the holy man who healed Eleri. Sten may have intended to live a quiet hermit life but The Maker Of All Things had other plans, this was his answer to Sten although it didn't dawn on him for a long time.

I was happy for Sten and if my part was unknown I was content.

The seasons came and went and I remained hidden and forgotten.

There came a time when Sten made it clear he wanted to be left alone for he was old and tired. He lay in his Kiffig on a much more comfortable bed than he had started with, sewed by his grateful flock and filled with the softest of down, and I felt compelled to appear to him. This took me by surprise for I had no idea he was even aware of me. Yet I stood beside his bed, he looked so weak now as I knelt beside him. He raised his hand towards me, I took it in mine.

"Sten, have you known about me all this time?"

He was too weak to speak and he simply smiled. I knew in that moment he had indeed known about me all along and that he was aware of what I had done for Eleri, and wanting to see me in person was the only way he could thank me.

He was completely at peace, he felt he had at last atoned for all the evil he had once done, he knew that his years of service were the answer The Maker Of All Things had given him. I felt a familiar presence behind me but didn't turn. Sten looked beyond me assured at last that his sins had been forgiven and quietly slipped away.

I knelt beside him for a moment while I could and through the soil summoned the people of the village. When they came they found only his body which they buried beside the Kiffig and mourned the passing of a holy man and a friend.

Chapter 18

Abbot Pierre

The earth rolled on and on around the sun in the endless dance of the universe. I was aware of a man standing on the bridge looking at the white house which by now was rather run down and used by the local farmers as a storehouse. He was a short squat man with grey hair that was shaved on the top. He had a simple white robe and a black scapular and held a long staff in his hand. He was a very devout man and it was time for him to say his devotions. He was wondering if he could rest in the white house just for a while and pray.

Somehow I was drawn to him but it was not him who drew me. I felt a familiar presence and knew that The Son Of The Maker Of All Things had spoken to him. He entered the enclosure and walked up to the door of the house, finding it slightly open he stepped in. And for some reason I was drawn to follow.

After his devotions he rested on a pile of straw just for a moment. Just for a moment but he was soon fast asleep.

I found I had taken on my physical form though I hadn't intended to, nor did I think this man whose name was Pierre even believed in my kind. I stood and watched Pierre for a while wondering why I was there when I became aware the Son was there too.

"He is a good man." He said.

"He is." I answered. "But why am I here?"

"I have work for him here and I need something from you."

I could never look directly at the Son and I found it difficult to ask him anything. So I stood and watched the old man sleeping and waited for the Son to explain, or not, I would just do his bidding whatever.

"You often get involved with people, Moonpool, but you have never done any harm."

This was a relief to hear considering some of my interfering and his silence at times, I felt I ought to point out a few things but he knew already.

"When he stirs, before he is fully awake, ask him to move the Abbey here."

"Why would he listen to me?"

"He will think you are Mary and that he has had a vision."

I was shocked. "No, no. I couldn't do that, it would be a deception."

"I didn't say you should pretend to be her. What he believes is entirely up to him. Just vanish once you have delivered the message."

"I can't, I just can't, surely it's wrong, but how can it be wrong when you ask? Why not get Mary to do it herself?"

"You know that those who have passed over do not come back."

"But …"

"Not even Mary."

"But …"

"Many of your kind who are less true than you will play tricks on people, and some who have turned to evil deliberately deceive, pretending to be the spirit of a loved one. So it is no great effort on your part to do this for me and for him."

"But …"

"This is no deception for you will not claim to be her. Sometimes people need a little help to decide to do the right thing. When he saw this place the idea had occurred to him anyway, he just needs confirmation, and he needs a reason to go back and tell his brothers to move here."

"Can't you tell him?"

"I have my reasons, Moonpool." I knew he was smiling.

"But …"

End of conversation. So all I could do was to wait. And while I waited I contemplated the contents of the house. There were sacks of grain and root vegetables, crates of apples, jars of ale, farming tools, rugs. The humans had come a long way since I first met Ban. So I waited until he began to stir as the first rays of the sun shone in through the slats in the eastern wall. In that dreamy half-awake state that comes after a refreshing sleep he gazed up at me and blinked.

"Pierre, I have a message for you from The Son Of The Maker Of All Things. He asks that you move your Abbey here."

He began to rise but I had gone by the time he got onto his knees.

A few days later Pierre returned with five and one other men dressed as he was. They went to the village first and offered to build another barn for storage in exchange for the white house by the river. They offered to help with all tasks on the land and had brought new farming techniques which they would share. The people of the village recognised that these were holy men and were more than happy with the offer, even offering help to build the barn and move the things. In a couple of days they had built a large barn outside the enclosure, moved all the stores into it and then took up residence in the white house. And when they had put it into good order Lord Rhys and Bishop Bernard of St David's came with great ceremony. Lord Rhys granted them all the surrounding lands and Bishop Bernard came to consecrate the house, designating it as an Abbey and to officially induct Pierre as Abbot.

At this time also The Maker Of All Things appointed the Messenger Sofiel to watch over the house.

Sofiel and I met in the early dawn at the entrance to the white house. Sofiel is an angel guardian dressed in white with wings folded behind and a sheathed sword on a belt of gold.

"This means my time here is over now." I said to Sofiel neither of us visible to the humans if they should happen to pass. "Now I can rest, now I will fall asleep."

"That is not the case. Unless the Almighty has told you otherwise, for he has sent me to watch over the house only and not the valley."

"He hasn't said anything but I know my time should be over, there is no room for me in Christianity."

"Roman Christianity you mean. That is more about the importance of humanity and an organised hierarchical structure. You are a nature spirit and you should know the importance of the natural world and that the

Almighty is in everything he has made. You are needed as much now as you have ever been. In fact I get the impression that you will be needed more in the future as Roman domination didn't end with the fall of the empire but lives on in the establishment of the church."

"I don't see how I could possibly be needed, you I can understand but not me."

"An established church is in danger of distancing itself from people and the natural world and the spiritual side of faith. Fortunately there are a great many individual Christians who are still close to what is important, but it is the individuals rather than the structured church. We are both here for a reason, mine is because of the spiritual, yours the natural."

"I wish I could hear from him. I fear I am blundering around as the humans do without understanding the consequences."

"Monapool."

The Son stood with us and we both cast our eyes down. He now used my Anglo-Saxon name when speaking to me.

"My Father placed you here for a reason and he doesn't change. Your place is here for all the time the Earth remains." He said.

I wondered at that, I would remain while the Earth remains.

"Sofiel may be a higher being than you but remember with us there is no hierarchy, my Father asked that all created beings call him Father and I lived on Earth to be a servant." He continued. "Pierre is human, a good and holy human but still a human and he will need both of you, for he will lay the foundation for something that will be part of this place from now on, he needs to lay a good foundation because as you know humanity is not always consistent. Sofiel can guide him in wisdom and holiness and Monapool in the needs of the land and the people who dwell here."

I wondered why he used my Anglo-Saxon name. Then I heard a movement behind us in the entrance of the house. Turning we saw Pierre on his knees.

"My Lord." He said quietly. "I will listen to them for the task is too great for me alone."

I looked at Sofiel and Sofiel looked at me, surprise on both our faces. We didn't know he was there and what the Son said was for him as much as for us, and we hadn't realised that we were both now visible.

Chapter 19

Steady Growth

Every morning before the sun came up Pierre stood in the entrance to talk to us. He was somewhat embarrassed that he had previously thought I was Mary, though not as embarrassed as I was, but he asked about the land and the best places for certain types of farming and he asked about the people, their history, their hopes and also their needs. I always left when he talked to Sofiel because that was to do with heavenly matters. But while the three of us were together I knew a peace that I had not known before, not even in the quiet long ages before I met Ban and the ice came and went over the surface of the land.

Sofiel is a being of pure spirit and yet can take on a form visible to humans at any time. In a sense the Sofiel Pierre and I see is not where Sofiel is but a presence from above. While I am a spirit bound by nature and where I am is where I am and my physical presence is of the earth as is the human presence. And yet the humans have a spirit they very rarely understand that is greater than either Sofiel or myself.

This spirit was very obvious in Pierre and through his own wisdom and the questions he asked us and his compassion for the people brought so many back to a faith in the Son.

He and his monks worked hard on the land and went about among the people of the valley caring for them in their troubles and illnesses. Every morning after Pierre had spoken to us he held a devotion in the house with his monks before sending them out into the communities, and on the Lord's Day they celebrated with bread and wine in all the small churches of the area.

The work of the monks both practical and spiritual was a tremendous benefit to the locality. The farms of the valley became very prosperous with their hard work, their new techniques and dare I say with my advice. The faith in Christianity grew daily and many young men and women begged to be allowed to join the order. Even when Pierre had sorted out those who were genuine the number of adherents grew too large for the small Abbey. And there was no place except in the village to cope with the growing number of pilgrims on their way to St David's.

Pierre was particularly keen to see us one morning. It was very early and as the days were getting short the sun had not yet risen.

"Sofiel, Monapool, I need your advice." He said.

"You always have our advice." Said Sofiel. "Although these days you probably don't need it."

"I believe it is time for me to move on. The good news is too great to keep it just here, I need to move on."

"I will miss you." I said. "The brothers are all good men but they do not have the depth of faith you do, none of them will seek me. But I am probably being a little selfish, and of course what you have begun here they are perfectly capable of continuing."

"I need to appoint a successor."

"Who do you have in mind?" Asked Sofiel.

"This was the advice I need. I was hoping you could suggest someone, Aiden would be the obvious choice."

"Aiden it is then, but why ask us." Said Sofiel.

"Because I am not sure, is he a good and spiritual man?"

"I am not a judge of the relationship between anyone and God, it is not my place." Admitted Sofiel.

"Monapool, you know people and sometimes you will express an opinion where, and I mean no disrespect, Sofiel won't."

"Aiden is a good, diligent worker and people like him, but like Sofiel I am not in a position to judge his spirituality."

Pierre seemed troubled. "And I suppose neither of you can comment on anyone else either."

"All the brothers are good men, hard-working and diligent, you have been a good leader, I cannot say any one man is better than the others." I said. "If I may express an opinion, after all it was what you were hoping for, I like Mark."

"But Mark is only a boy."

"It is only my opinion, from my perspective they are all boys."

"You are a good and spiritual man, Pierre." Said Sofiel. "You are in the best position to choose. Continue to pray, I am sure the Lord will lead you."

Pierre shook his head and sighed. "I suppose I am so happy here and things are going so well perhaps it is just that part of me would rather stay than start again somewhere else."

"Wherever you go you will succeed." I assured him. "We will watch over the people here."

"You have not told Aiden about us?" Asked Sofiel.

"Aiden has rigid beliefs, I suppose that is what makes him the ideal choice certainly as far as the order is concerned. He is not a dreamer or a visionary, just a solid Cistercian." He sighed. "I suppose that makes him the only choice to lead the brothers when I leave."

"I still like Mark." I couldn't help adding.

John of Torrington who owned much of the land, though how anyone can claim to own land I don't understand when the land is still there after they have died, was impressed by the work the monks were doing. He came to the white house with an offer for Pierre.

"I have wanted to come for a long time." He said. "I have heard so much about you and the good work your monks are doing."

"All we do is to the glory of God."

"I see you are rather cramped here."

"The people of the village are good. With their help we cope very well."

"I dare say, but wouldn't you prefer something larger?"

"Well, it is time I moved on for there are other places where I can take the good news. I am on the point of moving north with some of my brothers to begin a work there. This will not be too small then."

"And who will be in charge when you go?"

"Aiden will be Abbot here."

"And where will I find Aiden?"

"He went to St Brynach's this morning but I don't know if he will still be there."

"When are you going, and if there is anything you need just ask, I would like to help."

John left to find Aiden but I didn't follow, Pierre was in the process of gathering things together with four of the others, and I noticed Mark was one of them, for they were leaving that day and I wanted to say goodbye and assure him that I had spoken to the nature spirit of the area he was going to.

Chapter 20

New House

Aiden was a good man but he was worldlier than Pierre. John of Torrington had given him land some way up the Gronw not far from where the Roman outpost had been and was providing stone and labourers to build an Abbey to be proud of. Aiden was watching the dismantling of the old white house for the stones would be used somewhere in the new building. He was not sufficiently aware for me to appear and he didn't seem to be interested in Sofiel.

"I hope I will be able to live up to your standards Pierre." He said to himself, while the stones were carefully lifted onto the carts.

The earth turned a few more times and the old white house was gone. The people of the village were not at all happy with this and had got together and built a simple stone chapel on the site. Rhys, son of Sten, son of Eleri had seen to that. As the chapel was being built he stood at the entrance in the early morning before any of the villagers arrived to carry on with the work.

"Nature spirit, whoever you are." He said softly into the air.

"Rhys." I said softly back as I stood beside him.

He was a short, rather plump man with dark wavy hair and deep blue eyes that were prone to merriment. He was about to kneel.

"Don't do that, I am a servant of The Maker Of All Things. How do you know of me?"

"The old Hermit Sten told my father about you, but he didn't know your name."

"I am Pwll'euad in your tongue, Monapool in the Anglo-Saxon tongue."

"And this place is special to you."

"Yes, but not just to me, it has been a special place in the heart of the valley through all the ages."

"And I hope it will continue to be so. We are calling this place Hendy Gwyn Ar Daf as well as the village. I know it is not white stone but it is still a holy place as far as we are concerned. The new house will be far too grand for us."

"And will you keep the dedication to St Mary?"

"We could dedicate it to you."

"No, don't do that, it would just not be fitting, I am a pagan goddess." I smiled. "St Mary is a good dedication."

Meanwhile the new house was built and dedicated with much ceremony. From there the monks still worked hard and the valley continued to prosper. But Sofiel stayed in the small chapel by the river.

"Why are you still here?" I asked Sofiel.

"This is where the Almighty placed me. He hasn't moved me, any more than he has moved you, he doesn't forget things like that so there must be a reason."

"Do you know how Pierre is doing?"

"He has founded an abbey at Strata Florida and is doing well there. How is Aiden doing?"

I looked at Sofiel enquiringly. "You don't know."

"It is not my place, nor has a messenger been sent there."

"This doesn't sound good does it. However, he is doing well and the valley is prospering, the monks are hardworking and faithful and still increasing in number."

"You have met Rhys, or rather Rhys has met you."

"A family tradition. I hope I was not wrong in meeting with him."

"You have your own ways, Monapool, and they always seem to work out." And when Angels get a twinkle in their eye it really is a twinkle.

"Has he spoken to you?"

"Not a family tradition."

"I can introduce him to you if you wish."

Sofiel smiled an enigmatic smile, angels are hard to read, humans are much easier.

Pilgrims travelling to St David's and back still found the Old White House as it was called even if it wasn't white a fairly comfortable place to rest the night. Rhys made sure of that, making sure the straw beds were new straw and the blankets were clean and dry and there was bread and cheese and water on hand. And Sofiel watched over the place.

Occasionally a church dignitary would be on a pilgrimage but they always knew that they would be welcomed at the New White House where there were feather mattresses and meat and wine. Very often their pilgrimage was delayed a little due to the hospitality of the monks.

Rhys was sitting on the bridge waiting for the two pilgrims who were asleep in the house to wake.

"Monapool."

"Rhys." I sat beside him.

"I don't understand people. You have been around a long time do you understand them?"

I reflected a moment on all the people I have ever drawn close to. "I don't suppose I ever will but I suppose I do have a lot of experience."

"We are all equal in the sight of God. So why do some people go to the Abbey while everyone else comes here?"

"Don't worry about it. The Maker Of All Things sees. From what I understand of human nature those who come here he will actually receive a blessing and their pilgrimage will mean something because it is not easy. Make a pilgrimage too comfortable and it means nothing."

"Do you speak to God?"

"I talk to him but he rarely answers, I am not in his presence as the angels are, I am a creature of this world. You can speak to him you have a spirit that is closer to him than I am. You have a place in his plan, I am simply a guardian."

"But he has spoken to you."

"He speaks to both of us, not often but humans don't always recognise his voice. In that sense it is easier for me because I know his voice so well, you have so many voices in your heads mostly from your own needs and hopes."

"How do I recognise his voice?"

"I am a nature spirit. It is not my place to sort out things between you and The Maker Of All Things.

You must find your own way, all I can tell you is that his voice is never what you expect."

"Surely you can help me with this?"

"Ask Sofiel, the Angel who has a presence in the chapel and guards over the pilgrims."

"An Angel? That explains the presence I have felt and the lightness in there even when it is night. This Angel hasn't spoken to me."

"Then you had better stop talking to me, you need to learn to listen to The Maker Of All Things. I interfere far too much and it really isn't my place. You ask questions that are none of my business."

"So, what are you then? A pagan goddess, a guardian or a nature spirit?"

"I am a servant of The Maker Of All Things, he has placed me here as a sort of guardian but I still haven't worked out what that means. Besides, I interfere too much."

I looked at him, then I looked round at the valley, this might be my last time as I realised that I do need to distance myself from humanity. Then I looked at him again. "Goodbye Rhys. You are a good man and do not need me." And I was gone.

Chapter 21

Brother Andrew

It was early morning a few days after the spring equinox that I felt the pull of someone reaching out to he knew not what. A young monk stood in the grounds of St. Mary's, he was watching the rising of the sun through the break in the clouds. The small stone church which stood on the site as more befitting for the pilgrims that passed through. With all the different people coming to the valley through the ages there were still many of the indigenous people who could, had they known how, trace their bloodline back to Ban. This man could, I can always tell.

His was a peaceful soul and although he was a devout follower of the Way he was still grounded in the natural world and as such he was seeking something in the very nature of the valley.

"Whoever you are," He said into the air, "I will be spending a lot of time here. I have been appointed to see to the needs of the pilgrims who stay here and it would be good to have someone to talk to when there is no one else."

He waited for a while, then he picked up his pack and entered the church. I knew Sophiel would look after him. The monk would probably know the presence of an angel but would they talk I didn't know.

No pilgrims came for several days and the monk, apart from saying his daily offices inside, spent most of his time outside. Occasionally walking into the village for supplies, his family farmed in the hills to the north so he was well known, people were kind and were happy to supply his needs. Yet still he was lonely.

A group of pilgrims did arrive late one night. He fed them and provided bedding for them but they said very little to him for they were tired and just wanted to sleep. The next morning they set out early after a frugal breakfast and did talk about their expectations to reach St. Davids and wipe out some of their sins.

The monk sat on the western bank and watched the sun climb higher into the sky. He was so downcast I relented and sat with him. He was so lost in his thoughts he didn't notice me for a while.

He almost jumped when he did become aware of me. He stared at me for a moment before looking down at his hands.

"In case you are wondering I am called Monapool, though my name has changed a few times as the languages have changed."

He continued to look down at his hands, he was trembling.

"And you are…?"

"Andrew." He said when he had found his voice.

"No need to be afraid, Andrew. I am the valley and you have always lived here, you know me well enough now."

"It's just … well … I …"

"Don't say you didn't really believe I existed, I can only appear to you because you do."

"No ... yes ... er." He looked at me again and I held his gaze for a moment before he looked up at the surrounding hills.

"I always knew." He said somewhat calmer. "The old stories ... but you are not old."

"I was old before the first people came here."

"I ... well ... I never expected you to be so beautiful."

"And yet you live in this beautiful valley."

He looked at me again. Oh dear, he was young and my kind do have this glamour. I could see a crush coming on.

I jumped up and stood in front of him.

"Brother Andrew, you are follower of the Son, you should regard me as a pagan deity. Now, you are going to have to confess you misplaced feelings and erroneous beliefs to the Abbot. Who is the Abbot now anyway?"

"Cynan."

"He sounds Cymry. He hasn't come from across the sea this time."

"Politics, I don't get involved." Then he suddenly laughed, somewhat embarrassed. "And I apologise. Of course we are of different kinds, it would be improper. But can we talk from time to time? I will try to forget how beautiful you are."

"We can be friends." I sighed. "But I have had so many over the ages. I have a habit of getting involved with humanity, I suppose I am inquisitive and like to know what is going on."

"If you don't mind, I would like to hear about some of your friends."

"I know your family, Andrew, though that is not your given name. But why are you a monk here?"

"The monks of the Abbey have lived among us for so long, they have helped in so many ways, I suppose I was impressed by their lifestyle. Being a monk gives me purpose. For years pilgrims have stopped here on their way to St. David's and the Abbey felt it only right that they send someone from the order to care for their needs both physical and spiritual. So here I am. But your story must be far more interesting than mine."

In between the passing of pilgrims at times when Andrew was not in the village or visiting his family we sat together and discussed many things. I told him of some of the people I had known, beginning with Ban who I said he was descended from, and how the valley had changed over the years. He told me of his concerns for the Abbey, how because of the support of wealthy and influential people it was becoming very nationalistic, not a bad thing in itself but these were not settled times and the Abbey was not the place to play politics. We did not talk of matters of faith, I told him it was not right for me to interfere.

The Abbey grew in importance, Lord Rhys paid homage to Henry the Second there and many important, at least to the humans, people were buried there.

But more important to me was the fields behind St. Mary's, or Eglwys Fair, the villagers organised an annual fair there. It reminded me of so many events that had taken place on that site over the years. The seasons came and went, pilgrims passed back and forth, Andrew took care of their needs diligently, he had found his purpose in life. And each year the fete filled the field and it looked so full of life and jollity. One year Andrew, now much more mature, asked me if I would like to attend and I willingly joined him.

The sights and sounds, the people selling all sorts of produce and clothing, the stalls where people could throw hoops or balls at targets, the groups of musicians, the bunting and streamers, nothing much had changed. The smell of cooking pervaded the place. There were musicians and jugglers, even a fortune teller who I avoided.

"We had some important visitors at the Abbey last week." Said Andrew, obviously quite excited.

"Important?"

"The Archbishop of Canterbury and Gerald his clerk, and he is a well-known historian. The Abbey here is famous."

"Oh." Was all I said. "We have had some very interesting pilgrims visit us here."

Human rank and position don't mean anything to me and I think Andrew was rather deflated by my obvious lack of interest.

"I never thought to ask." Said Andrew as we passed a stall selling meat pies. "Do you eat?"

"I can, but I never have, I have no need."

"Would you like to try something?"

"Not really. I am spirit and will never be human out of choice so I would rather not."

"Brother Andrew!" Called another monk. "So now I know who you have been hiding down here."

"Brother Paul, this young lady is a friend of my family, she lives in the valley."

"Pleased to meet you, and your name is?"

"Monapool."

"Monapool, that is a very unusual name. And what is your family."

I waved my arms to indicate everyone and everything around. "This is my family."

"You are a dark horse Andrew, is this something the Abbott should know about."

"He already does, I keep nothing from him." 'Except who she really is.' He thought.

"Will you be telling him you are showing her around the fair?"

"I don't need showing around, I have been to so many fairs." I said.

Sadly Andrew was sent to Strata Florida soon after this. Paul took on his responsibilities of looking after pilgrims in St Mary's. He asked in the village for Monapool but no one had heard of me, not by that name anyway, maybe if he had asked for Pwll'euad he would have found out. Since he wasn't aware of who I really was I couldn't have appeared to him even if I had wanted to, which I didn't. So I was content to settle back into obscurity.

Chapter 22

The Dreamer

A young girl was sitting on the bridge by the church on a sunny afternoon. She was day dreaming about the stories her grandmother had been telling her, stories of a nature spirit who used to live in the valley, stories that had been passed down through the family. She was watching the swirling of the water trying to imagine the nature spirit. I must admit I am drawn to children because they have not learned not to believe, and this girl was so sure of the existence of the spirit she was willing very hard to see me.

If only I knew what I was supposed to do. I had innocently got Andrew into trouble, another example of interfering too much and getting too close to someone. But this was a simple girl who had nothing to do with the Abbey, maybe I could risk it?

"Hello Carys." I sat beside her.

A moment of surprise was quickly surpassed by a look or sheer joy. She was so overcome she couldn't speak.

I felt very young again, it was her belief that enabled me to take on human form and I always gain something from that belief.

"My name is Pwll'euad." Celtic was still the predominant language of the local people.

"Oh, oh, I am so happy to see you." She beamed. "But how do you know me?"

"In the village you are known as 'The Dreamer' because you always have your head in the clouds and never concentrate on what you are doing."

"Will you come into the village so I can show them you are real? They wouldn't make fun of me then."

She so reminded me of Sunlight who I had taught so many years ago that not only was I willing to go with her but I felt perhaps I could teach her the old teachings too. Perhaps this was for me rather than for her, but I still believed it couldn't hurt. It all seemed so strange though. The simple village of Pentreban with its round houses was called Whiteland or Hendy Gwyn Ar Daf depending on the language and these were now outnumbered by the square houses which were all cramped together.

"Carys, where have you been." Called a woman rushing out her door, a worried look on her face.

"Oh Mam, I have been looking for Pwll'euad and I found her."

"Pwll'euad?" She looked enquiringly at me. "Why were you looking for her? Excuse me but do I know you? I seem to have heard your name from somewhere but I don't think I know you. I hope Carys hasn't been bothering you."

I couldn't help smiling. This reminded me so much of Sunlight and her mother.

"Hello Mair." I said. "I have always been here."

"We don't mix much with the people up the hill, are you from there."

"From there as much as anywhere, I do tend to move around."

"So, who are your family?"

"I suppose my closest family are in the Velfey area." For, if I count Little Rainbow as my daughter they are the ones mostly descended from her.

"Can you show us some magic?" Carys asked.

"No, not this time. I am the past, you are the present and the future."

By now a few people had gathered. My clothing was unusual and the name Pwll'euad had a resonance in their memories. They knew there was something special about me but only Carys knew. It was enough that I was known by her, I didn't want to interfere with too many people.

"Well, Pwll'euad," Said Mair. "You will stay for a bite to eat now you are here."

"I would be honoured to, you are most kind."

Mair invited me and her neighbours into her simple home and as I sat quietly with Carys I heard much local news.

I heard of wars, some of the local men were away fighting, the unrest that was caused because of the Abbey's allegiance with a remote king and his dignitaries.

"Because of the Abbey we cannot avoid the war here, they do not represent the local people." Said Mair. "What do you think, Pwll'euad? You say you have always been here."

"Everything was a lot simpler before, I knew who I was protecting and why. I sense a great danger and I do not know if I should get involved yet I cannot simply stand by."

All eyes were on me in stunned silence. I looked at their surprised faces. They didn't understand what I meant and I wondered if I had said too much.

"Who are you really?" Asked an old woman with a penetrating gaze but a closed mind so I couldn't work out what was behind the question.

"A friend."

I could sense that these people were afraid of the war coming to their village. The Abbey was an important Abbey and had drawn unwanted attention to the area, while all that the villagers wanted was to be left in peace to get on with their lives. They were all silent, looking at me expectantly.

"The people of the Abbey have made their choice, my role is to protect you who live in the valley. You do not need to know how." I said.

"Protect us?" Asked Mair. "You don't look old enough to protect us and you are a woman. I suppose you have important connections then, perhaps with some of the nobility?"

"I do have connections."

Everyone seemed somewhat relieved by this. The old woman smiled a knowing smile.

Although it was remote the small stone hut at Cyffig had been replaced by a small church by the local farmers because they didn't always fit in with the villagers of Whiteland. Silverwheel and I had often met at the site before and on occasions we still did.

"Moonpool." Said Silverwheel. "Why do you worry so much about whether you are doing the right thing?"

"What makes you think I am worried?"

"You wanted to see me didn't you?"

I smiled, we knew each other so well.

"You and I have seen so much, so many changes, so much fighting." She said. "Yet still the humans still increase and your valley is still here. Whether you do the right thing or the wrong thing is not going to make a difference, it never has."

"I suppose you are right. But I do wonder at times what would have happened here if I had become human."

"Only The Maker Of All Things knows that."

"But our time is over, this is their time."

"Yet we are still here, we should make the most of everything, enjoy what there is to enjoy. The humans are the ones making the mistakes, look at the wars that happen all the time."

"Then I will enjoy Carys' company and I will protect the villages in the valley as much as I can."

"And I will travel the world and talk to your brothers and sisters wherever they still are."

"Have many fallen asleep or become human?"

"Some, most of us are still here and do what we can even though hardly anyone takes notice any more. You are not alone, Moonpool, so you carry on doing what you always do."

So, whenever Carys came to the bridge and sat I sat with her. I told her about nature, the plants, the trees, the river, the hills, the journey of the sun and moon, the stars and some of their stories. I told her about the herbs and their uses, I told her about the lives of the animals down to the smallest creatures and the birds soaring in the sky. She wanted to know about my story too so I told her of some of the people I had met through the ages and the battles I had helped with. I enjoyed my time with her but always I felt a tension in the air.

Then they came, a band of men on horses entered the valley from the east. I went to the edge of the village prepared to get the horses to turn aside since they would listen to me even if the men didn't. But they turned aside anyway and rode up to the Abbey and I was prevented from following. So I had to wait where I was. I knew blood was shed, I could feel it in the soil.

When they left I was still unable to go there. But the danger to any of the villages had passed, whatever this was it was with the Abbey alone. I sought Carys and found her in her mother's house.

Without thinking I just appeared. Mair stared open mouthed.

"Pwll'euad. What is happening, we heard a large number of knights were coming, is it true?"

"It is true, but they have come and gone, they went to the Abbey but I don't know what happened there."

"You stopped them coming here then?"

"No, they weren't coming here at all."

"Tad works at the Abbey."

She was so afraid, I had to try and get there. This time I was allowed. I was stunned, some of the workers in the cemetery had been killed and Iwan, Carys' father was only slightly wounded. All the monks had been beaten and some of them quite badly wounded. I returned to Carys and her mother with the news.

"Your Tad is wounded but he is alright. I don't know what that was about but all the monks were beaten."

My sudden disappearance and reappearance startled Mair again. I just thought it best not to try to explain, let her sort it out in her own mind.

Carys came and hugged me.

"Your Mam needs a hug Carys."

She hugged her startled mother, the relief they both felt was wonderful to see.

And I was gone.

Being spirit is all very well but sometimes I need a physical presence to feel and now I needed a human heart to ask something. So I took on human form by St. Mary's church while no one was around.

"O Maker Of All Things, why did you stop me from going to the Abbey?"

"The attackers had iron swords, you would have been killed."

Would have been killed, not might have been killed. Fading and falling asleep I had contemplated and I would be content with that as my essence would sink back into the valley, the idea of being killed was a shocking thought because did I have an eternal soul like the humans? I couldn't ask because I knew the answer, it was not for me to know.

The next day Carys was on the bridge again so I sat with her. We didn't speak for some time, just sat and watched the swirling water. She had changed, grown, the innocence had died in her.

"Why did they have to attack the Abbey, why kill some of my father's friends? What is wrong with people?"

"Jealousy, greed, power. It is all pointless anyway. What is hard is that you have to see it at your age, you should be happy and carefree."

"Why are there such evil people in this world that they want to fight and kill?"

"In everything I have seen, even among my own kind, it is one thing I will never understand. But always remember there is far more good, most people are good people, you have loving parents and kind neighbours, remember that."

She sat and thought for a long time and we both watched the swirling water.

"You said it is one thing you don't understand, are there others?"

"Time, I still don't understand time. The plan of The Maker Of All Things, I don't understand that, nor do I understand how despite everything he still loves everyone. And what I am supposed to do, I don't understand that either."

"Can we be friends for always?"

I took hold of her hand in both of mine. "Friends never stop being friends."

I couldn't promise always because always for her was a long time while it passes so briefly for me. I was glad to have a friend again now.

"Did your mother say anything about me after I popped in and out like that?"

"She said, 'so who exactly is your friend?' and I said you were the nature spirit of the valley. Then all she said was 'oh'."

"You wanted me to do some magic before, I couldn't really do it then because I am not supposed to interfere with people. You are different, you have a depth of belief that few have these days. Do you still want to see some magic?"

"Seeing you pop in and out like that was magic enough. I am happy just to be with you and to talk."

As the Earth danced around the Sun Carys grew to be a wise woman. She married a nice young man from Velfrey who was a practical person and still regarded Carys as 'The Dreamer' so never was able to see me. He made sure their children were sensible too. But Carys would still come to the bridge and sit with me at times.

When Carys died I could not take on human form and had to mourn as best I could in spirit form.

Chapter 23

Great Pestilence

I was content to fade, the world had become too violent, too complicated. Until a man was fervently praying is St Mary's chapel. His hands grasped firmly on the rough stone altar, tears streaming down his face. Sofiel called to me and we stood together behind the distraught man, I could take on human form because the Angel willed me to, but I wondered why. The radiance of Sofiel lit the chapel so the man stopped and slowly and very cautiously turned his head. Seeing us both there he fell rather awkwardly onto the floor.

"Brother Mark." Said Sofiel gently. "The Lord has heard you and has seen the depths of love you have for his people. Stand, we are both servants of the Most High you should not fall at our feet."

Slowly and cautiously Brother Mark got to his feet.

"Tell me." Said the Angel. "What is it you ask?"

Still half sobbing Brother Mark said haltingly. "I know the Great Pestilence is coming, I don't know how to protect my people. There are holier men than me all around the world and no one has been able to stop it."

"The Great Pestilence will come and there is little you can do but be with them. I have asked Monapool to be here with you, she will be unaffected by the Pestilence and has knowledge of healing and herbs, if she is willing."

I looked into Sofiel's peaceful face. "Of course I am willing."

"Brother Mark." Said Sophiel quite sternly. "I know you have unwavering faith in The Almighty, You need to have faith in Monapool, without that she can do nothing. You need to know she is not an angel but she is still a spirit and much closer to nature than I am and understands people much better too. Only you need to know this, to everyone else she is a healer that you have asked to come here. Do you believe in her?"

"Yes." Mark looked rather puzzled, he didn't understand where I fit in but he was willing to believe because I was here, standing with an Angel, and if an Angel was willing to vouch for me then he could accept me.

"She appears to you now on my authority, but she can only retain her physical form by your belief. You need her so you need to believe in her. I will hand her over to you now."

I could feel the angel's authority to have me there withdrawn but I remained where I stood. Since my ability to take on human form comes from the belief of a human I do tend to reflect that person in some way while still being myself, I suddenly felt such compassion for the people of the village, so much more than I usually do, the strength of emotion made me weep with Mark. He saw the tears roll down my face and reached out to touch my cheek.

"Thank you Monapool." He said. "I see you understand and feel as I do, I gratefully accept your help even if I do not understand who you are."

Sophiel withdrew and the chapel seemed dark.

"Where do we start?" He asked.

"The Pestilence has not come here yet so we have some time, I must gather herbs, you can go about the people and try to get them to wash their homes out. But you must be aware, we will not be able to stop it, our only hope is to save as many people as we can, we will still have a lot of deaths and must prepare ourselves for that."

I gathered large quantities of thyme, sage and wild marjoram which I cut up and put into the water in each house as the people washed and scrubbed, following Mark from house to house. Then we went to the other villages in the valley and all the outlying farms.

"What about Arberth and Corvus?" Asked Mark.

"I am spirit of this valley, I could ask the spirits of those places but really it is up to them and if there are people of faith there. Much as I would like to I am somewhat bound, it is part of the responsibility The Maker Of All Things has given me."

"Then let us go to the Abbey."

So we set out towards the Abbey but a sudden coldness came over me apart from a burning in my arm from an old wound that never usually bothered me.

"I cannot go on." I said, shivering and holding my arm. I tried one more step but the pain brought me to my knees.

"What is it?" Mark was most concerned.

"Iron, do they iron there, swords or anything?"

"They need to protect themselves, the brothers don't use them but many of the lay people have them. And there is iron on many of the fixtures and fittings. Why should iron affect you so much?"

"It is the way with my people. You take the water and the herbs, I cannot." I crawled back and the pain ebbed and I breathed easily, then waved him on. "Go, I will be fine."

I did not fully understand, the local people use iron tools and it never bothers me, it had to be the swords.

He began to walk on, looking back briefly to see that I was alright, I smiled back and got to my feet.

"Go, I have other things to collect." I shouted.

While Mark went to the Abbey I collected as much honey as I could, I picked a large amount of cowleek, also more thyme and wild marjoram. I went to the home of Delyth and asked if I could use her stove. I boiled the herbs and filled as many pots as I could find.

Mark returned rather despondent.

"I tried." He said as he sat watching me fill the pots. "But the Abbot accused me of implying that they were filthy."

"Well, I hope they are clean enough, I suppose it is likely that the Abbey is, I am sure the monks work hard at scrubbing floors and washing bowl as much as they work hard in the fields."

"The Abbey itself, but many of the men who work there live in hovels, I tried to speak to them and left your special water with them, we can only hope they will listen to my advice."

Word spread that the pestilence had reached Caerfyrddin. It would soon reach here, so we kept watch over the health of the villagers. I gathered together a small group of older women who offered to help. The first sign of a fever the sufferer was given honey, the moment a swelling bled they were bathed with my mixture, the vomiting and diarrhoea cleaned and the patient washed. I could go from house to house instantly and take some of the fever and the pain from people but I cannot prevent death. The band of women worked tirelessly and seemed unaware of my appearances and disappearances. We worked for days as more and more people became ill, some of the people began to recover and get stronger but sadly we could not save everyone. The women grew tired and I had to insist that they went home to sleep even if it was a few at a time. Mark worked harder than everyone, and on top of that he went to the bedside of those who were dying to pray and give them the last rites. Miraculously none of my women volunteers, nor Mark, caught the pestilence.

Day after day we tended the sick and the dying, feeling the relief whenever anyone recovered making sure they ate to build up their strength. But too many died, far too many. I lost track of time, I was never very good at that anyway, but eventually fewer people were getting sick. Yet it was still some time before we knew the danger had passed.

The villages of the valley had survived and it was time to mourn the dead. The bodies of the dead were burned outside each village and a mound was raised over each site.

Mark held a requiem mass in St Mary's chapel and many of the relatives of the deceased attended and it gave them some comfort.

After the service as people made their way home, Mark stood outside and they thanked him as they passed. I had been waiting outside through the service and when the last person left he turned to me, he was worn out, thin and drawn.

"You need to rest." I told him. "And you need to mourn all those we couldn't save, especially your parents."

"And what about you? You look unchanged so I assume you don't need to rest, but do you need to mourn?"

"As I am I have a human heart and I will mourn, I do as spirit too but it is not as intense, so I will retain this form for a few days so I can mourn properly. I have seen too many people die and even though I know they are received into the Otherworld I still feel the loss."

"You did not come to the requiem."

"It is complicated, I am on a different spiritual level I cannot explain, I draw strength from The Maker Of All Things without the need for ceremony. It may sound like boasting but it is not."

With the mention of ceremony a thought occurred to him. "We have not heard from the Abbey."

One old lady coming from behind me grabbed my hand. "Monapool, thank you for all you have done, surely you are an angel."

"No, Mabli, I am not an angel. You and your friends did as much as I did. If only we could have saved many more."

"We are all old and have had the best parts of our lives, you are young and if you had caught the pestilence and died that would be a waste of all you could be."

"I am already all I could be."

"While we were tending the sick I saw you come and go, you suddenly appeared and disappeared, I was too busy at the time to think about it but now I have time to reflect I have to ask who are you?"

"Someone who cares for the people of the valley."

"I think I know, Monapool is Pwll'euad in our language." She kissed my hand and went on her way.

Mark smiled at her retreating figure. He really did look worn out, he could go on no longer.

"Rest tonight, Brother Mark, and tomorrow, the next day will be soon enough to go to the Abbey and find out how they fared." I said to him.

I stayed a while longer outside the chapel when everyone had gone. I may not be human but in this form I did actually feel tired myself and I was able to mourn the loss of so many who I should have been able to protect. As the sun began to set I let go of my physical presence.

In the quiet of the next morning I knew Mark would be sound asleep so I took on human form and with it the weight of sorrow at the death of so many. I entered the little church.

Sofiel appeared and said gently. "You know you could remain spirit and save yourself so much grief."

"I could, but those who died deserve my grief."

"I understand, you would not be the nature spirit you are if you did otherwise. I too grieve in my way but I am more aware of their free spirits in paradise. So perhaps I grieve for the loss of those who remain."

"If I were really human I would envy you Sofiel."

"And if I were human I would envy you Monapool. It is fortunate neither of us is human and do not envy. You and I have our places in God's order and his plan is always perfect."

In the evening of the second day Brother Mark came to the chapel hoping to find me, so I waited for him just outside the door.

"Ah, Monapool, I was hoping you would be here." He said. "They lost a lot of good people at the Abbey, it will be a long time before they can recover properly."

"And you, Mark, what will you do now?"

"The Abbot has commanded me back to help at the Abbey, there will not be any pilgrims for a long time so I am not needed here, while they need everyone they can get there."

"I will miss you, I still cannot go to the Abbey. Thank you for believing in me."

"My faith has been tested in many things, but my faith in you has been well placed."

"Your faith in The Maker Of All Things is still well placed, we just don't understand his plans. If it helps Sofiel doesn't either, but I don't suppose it does."

Chapter 24

Ladies Circle

Mabli and her friends came to the chapel a few days later. The sun had just set and there was a new moon in the sky. They stood looking up at the moon and wishing, wishing to see me.

A wish on the new moon, how could I possibly refuse. So I silently stood with them and also looked up at the moon. They were so intent in looking up and wishing they didn't notice me at first.

"We knew you would come Monapool, we only had to wish on the new Mona (The word for the Moon at that time)." Said Mabli when she suddenly realised I was standing with them. "We have been talking and we agree, we know who you are. You are the spirit of the valley."

"And some of us remember the stories that have been handed down." Said Bethan. "You are Pwll'euad."

I couldn't help smiling and I took hold of Mabli's and Bethan's hands. There was such love and respect in their combined belief in me it made me quite emotional and I could not help a tear or two.

"Come to my house." Said Mabli. "I have some fairly reasonable ale and good wholesome cake."

So I followed them and was soon sitting in a small, cramped room with five and one women. I had a mug of ale placed in one hand and a large piece of fruit cake in the other.

"Monapool or do you prefer Pwll'euad." Said Mabli.

"Monapool sounds better." I said. "But I had a different name before, it always means the same though so you call me whatever you wish."

"We have come together as a ladies circle to help the village recover. We were hoping that you would be willing to help us."

"If I can help in any way I would only be too glad to, the care of the valley is my concern."

"We have lost so many people in the village, I lost a son who was working up at the Abbey. His wife Myfanwy is the daughter of Gwawr," She nodded to a little woman tucked into the corner, "but she is very weak still. I wonder if you could help look after their little boy Dylan for her, only during the day, he will come to me in the evening."

"And I have a granddaughter, Nia, who lost both her parents, could you look after her as well?"

Soon I had a list of five and five children who the ladies circle hoped I could look after. This sounded like fun so I readily accepted. Children always make me feel young.

The next morning I was in the chapel with all these children of different ages, but they were all quiet. The pestilence had killed many parents, many of their friends too, and they were frightened and sad. Sophiel kept out of this, saying it was more in my line, children have their own angels.

How do I start? The children I had dealings with before were always happy, how do I help children who were grieving? Especially as I was grieving too. I could only be myself, nature is a good healer and nature was outside.

"If you will all follow me outside for a moment I want you to see something."

Silently they followed.

The sun was quite high in the sky and I stood facing them with the sun behind them. Then, because of their simple belief, I opened my wings wide so the sun could glint off them. I must say I am very proud of my wings, huge butterfly wings, dark and in places transparent and quite spectacular with the sun on them. The sad faces turned to expressions of wonder.

"Are you an angel?" Asked Nia.

"No I am not, but I can tell you this, you are standing in a gateway."

"A gateway?" Asked Rhian.

"A gateway to the Otherworld. From here although you cannot see them you are closest to your friends and family who you have lost. Come here when you want to talk to them and they will hear you even if you cannot hear them, and you will know they are safe and happy."

I folded up my wings.

"If you are not an angel, what are you and how do you know this?" Asked Dylan.

"Come back into the chapel and I will tell you."

So starting with my first meeting with Ban I told my story, the story of all my friends and how I lost them one after another. I told them about Little Rainbow, the hardest thing I had ever done, and I couldn't help but cry as I did, and I told them how I saw her bright and young taken into the Otherworld when she died. And I told them of all my friends over the ages and that I knew The Maker Of All Things and his Son had taken them to himself.

And they came to me in one large cwtch and we all cried together. The tension lifted, even I found this a release of all the sadness that I had carried with me for so long.

Slowly and reluctantly they went to their homes for the night.

The next day the ladies circle came with the children.

"Monapool." Began Mabli, she found it hard to talk through her emotions. "We can only thank you again, we heard some of the things you told them, and we ask that you continue to look after the children while we look after the village. If we are not imposing on you too much."

"I am more than happy to look after them. Can I take them wherever I want?"

"Most certainly you can, they need to get out and about."

"Then return to the village, we are all going for a walk."

So, over the next few days, I took them out into the fields and woods and taught them about the trees and the flowers, the birds and the animals. Over the days to follow as the moon went through her phases over and over I taught them about the seasons and planting and growing. I taught them about herbs and healing. I let them run and play and laugh and cry. After the horrors they had witnessed they needed to be children again.

I sat with them one at a time and let them talk, they talked of their sadness and loss and their fears, I would hold them as they wept and I wept with them. Slowly we all began to heal, the horrors and the loss would stay with them but they could now live.

Many of the ladies circle came to me as well, and then other villagers, and people from the other villages in the valley, and I listened to them all. If asked I said I was simply a good listener who had some experience, I kept from them who I really was, I felt it was important for them not to know, apart from the few who already did.

'Oh, Maker Of All Things, I thank you for this time. For once I do not feel I have been interfering.'

And I knew he was smiling.

Very early one morning while it was still dark, before the children had arrived, I stood outside the chapel and watched the stars and listened to them sing, Brother Mark came and stood beside me.

"How are things at the Abbey?" I asked.

"We do not have enough people to do all the tasks so we are all worn out. I have been sent to get some of the villagers to come and help."

"Help? There are not enough people here to do all the tasks, soon it will be harvest and many of the crops will not be brought in."

"I did try telling the Abbot. I will go back and tell him again. But it was a good reason for me to come and see you again and ask how things are."

"I am teacher of children. But soon, as they grow, they will have to work. There have been some joining of couples and, they don't know it yet, there will be babies.

There have been some deaths as well, we may be over the worst but the pestilence is not completely gone. The village is struggling but it will survive, and the same is true of the other villages in the valley. They will get through the next winter although it will be hard and I am content. I have seen humans survive and thrive through harder times than this, the sorrow and the loss will be the hardest for them to bear."

The sky in the cast began to brighten, it was going to be a good day.

"You do look tired, Brother Mark."

"I am, and I am considering leaving the order. I yearn for a simple life where I am not told what to do."

If he wanted my advice he didn't ask and even if he had I would not give it. He looked steadily at me for some time, then turned away shaking his head. I knew had feelings for me, he was not really destined for the monastic life, he did need to leave, get married and have a family. There were many girls in the village who had lost husbands, he would be made very welcome here, or up in Llanboidy or the Velfrey's.

Not many days passed and he left the Abbey and settled with a young widow in a farm up the Marlais. In time they had two healthy boys. My children grew and slowly left me to work in the fields. More babies were born and slowly the villages began to recover.

When all the children had left me I visited the last few who remained of the ladies circle to say goodbye. They had worked hard and had kept everyone together. They were sad that I was leaving, except I would always be there only not physically, and thanked me for all I had done. But all I asked was that they continued to pass on the stories about me so that I wouldn't be forgotten. Although it didn't really matter if I was forgotten, this time had been so special for me that if I did nothing else I had been here for a reason.

And I was gone.

Chapter 25

The Rebellion

Nia, now a grandmother herself, came and stood outside the chapel. The dawn had just broken and it was the spring equinox, the sky was blue and a gentle breeze ruffled the fresh green leaves. Such was her earnestness to see me again, and I will admit I wanted to see her as well, that I stood beside her quietly for a while before I spoke.

"Nia, it is a long time."

"For me, yes, but I see it is not for you." She studied me for a long time. "But I suppose you do not age."

"It depends on what you mean, I age in the sense that I experience the changes that happen, but I am already older than the world."

She looked a bit startled by that. Then she smiled. "I have been thinking over all the things you taught us children."

"Those were sad days."

She sighed. "But you made them happy."

"You wanted to see me, Nia, and it wasn't just to talk about those days."

"No. Our Village Elder was hoping to talk to you, he needs your advice."

"I will talk to him but I don't know about advice. This is not my time and I have interfered too much in the past. Still I will meet him here tomorrow."

The next day I was quietly watching the sun come up, breathing in the fresh, cool air, listening to the birds singing in the trees, the wind rustling the leaves of the trees, when I felt him approach.

"Monapool."

"Dylan." I turned. "You have grown to be a very wise leader."

"I had a good teacher."

"How are things in the villages of the valley?"

"It was hard for many years, only now we should be content to be getting on with things in peace."

"Ah, I see you are troubled, it is about Owain ap Gryffydd's revolt against the English."

"We cannot keep out of it, not even here, even the Abbott has sided with him."

"Everything is complicated now. Everything seems to be about who wants to be in charge and who can raise the largest army. I don't know what advice you expect me to give."

"You have fought for our valley before, you kept the peace with the Romans. Surely there is something you can do now."

"I advised the people to make peace with the Romans, and perhaps I scared them a little, if they hadn't I could not have prevented bloodshed. I am sorry but I cannot help now. I am the valley and I am nature, I have no authority over the hearts and minds of people."

"You have powers to protect us here."

"Here, well I can try to instil peace as I have always done, I can add strength to the defenders if the battle came here. But your concern is not just here is it?"

"Many of our young men want to join his army, they dream of the glory of the fight and upholding the pride of our nation."

"And you cannot stop them."

"No, but perhaps ..."

"I cannot change their determination, I never have been able to stop people coming or going, I couldn't stop the young people leaving before even if it had meant the end of the village. And I cannot go with them and help to fight with them. I know I have done so in the past but that was to protect the people from ruthless invaders. This is about who rules from afar. I will protect this valley and I will keep the peace here as long as those who live here let me, that is all I can do."

Dylan was more than disappointed, he was angry with me.

Nia came again the next day. It was overcast, a storm was brewing. I really didn't want to get involved but Nia called my name over and over.

"Dylan is not happy is he?" I said suddenly, startling her.

"I am sorry Monapool, Dylan feels powerless, how can he be Village Elder when the young men will not listen."

"They would not listen to me either."

"I know, they have made their minds up. Today they leave for the rebellion. We have lost too many people already and families will have to mourn again, fighting is such a waste of life."

"I have seen too much of that. But I cannot blame you humans, it has happened with my kind too, and with the angels. We can wish The Maker Of All Things had made this a peaceful world but he has not and we do not understand. We are all learning."

"Do you mind if I visit from time to time?"

"Not at all."

The earth circled many years while the rebellion continued. When Nia died I was content to exist as spirit only. I still watched the valley but while battles waged elsewhere no trouble came here. Not to any of the villages anyway, when it was over soldiers marched into the Abbey. They arrested the Abbot and some of the monks and took them back to Caerfyrddin and put them in prison. A new Abbot was appointed, years later he was arrested too, many of the possession taken, and then he was pardoned and returned. With all my long association with humans I will never understand them.

Chapter 26

Restored Faith

I was content to keep out of things, because they were left alone the villages were doing well at last but there always seemed to be some sort of trouble at the Abbey. Pilgrims were passing through on their way to St David's and a new monk was put in the chapel to look after them.

Brother Stephen stood at the entrance to the chapel. There was a light drizzle and he drew his cloak round him.

"Moonpool." He called into the air.

(Author's note: Mona had now been replaced by Moon in English. Although I have from the beginning used her name Moonpool it is a translation of her original name in a language that is no longer used, but Moonpool is the name she first spoke to me and of all the names she has been known by it is her favourite and I have used it at her request.)

Startled by what is now what my name had become I couldn't help but appear to him.

"Moonpool." I said to him, enjoying the sound of it. "I was told once by the spirit of the Moon that my last name would be the prettiest of them all and she was right."

I am sure that Silverwheel smiled at this.

"Brother Stephen." I said. "You wanted to see me?"

"My great-grandmother knew you so I am told, a lot of stories have been passed down the family, and now that I am here I wanted to meet you too."

"Yes, Nia was a good friend. But it is more than inquisitiveness that you wanted to see me is it not."

"Yes, it is. I try to be true to my faith and devout in my prayers, but I fear that not everyone at the Abbey is ... well, I have heard things."

"I never have had much to do with the Abbey, I am the valley and I am nature, I cannot get involved in religious matters."

"It isn't just about the Abbey. I find it hard to pray, I am not sure God hears me. You are the only spirit I can talk to and who will answer."

"No, I am not. I am a nature spirit, I am a lesser being than the angels. If it is a matter of belief I am not the one you should be talking to, I only distract you from your faith in The Maker Of All Things."

"But God doesn't answer."

"His answer is approaching, look."

Before he could say any more a group of people were approaching, three men and two women. Their clothes were worn and they were tired.

"This is Eglwys Fair in Whitland?" One of the men asked, a man with greying hair and wispy beard.

"Yes, and I am Brother Stephen. I take it you are pilgrims on your way to St David's and wish to stop here the night."

"And I am Edward." He reached out and grasped Stephen's forearm as he began to stumble.

I was not there now, this was between Stephen and the pilgrims. I know Stephen took them in to the chapel and quickly rushed to the village for bread and cheese and milk. Late into the evening they told him their stories and why they were going to St David's but I kept away.

Instead I sat on a bank outside Cyffig and sought Silverwheel.

It was getting dark and the Moon shone in the sky while Silverwheel shone on the bank beside me. I often wonder what local people thought when they saw her light in the distance.

"Moonpool." She said. "Are you happy with the name."

"Yes, thank you. But what is your name now?"

"My home is called Moon which is not my name but I have so many names all over the world. In English my old name that you know me by would be Silverwheel, but no one calls me that any more, nor do they use any of my older names they knew me by. What is worse is that people talk about the man in the moon and we both know there is no man it is just people think they see a face. In parts of the world some see a boy and a girl with a pale of water and other places they see a hare." She shrugged.

"Then between us you are Silverwheel."

She smiled and we sat in silence for a while.

"We both wish for the simpler days." She said at length, knowing me so well she knew my thoughts. "You are fortunate that the larger collections of people are a long way from your valley so stories about you have been passed down through families and are still believed and you are remembered."

"I am grateful for that, and I am glad that I have been able to help at times. However I was almost put in a difficult situation just now."

"Oh? Someone hasn't got a crush on you again have they?"

"Not this time. Stephen was having a crisis of faith and he sought me rather than The Maker Of All Things or his Son simply because of those legends that have been passed down. It is not my place to sort out faith matters and I cannot come between a human and the Son."

"You will just have to keep away from him, hard though that will be for him. I have seen the harm that is done when our kind get involved in such matters."

"I don't think there will be a problem, a group of very devout pilgrims arrived and they can help him because of their belief. I don't think he will need to talk to me anyway, at least I hope so."

"They are always best at sorting such things out between themselves, they understand each other better than we do."

He didn't need to talk to me but one day he was alone, standing at the entrance of the chapel, the sun shining in a clear blue sky.

"Moonpool." He called.

I was reluctant to appear but he called again.

"Moonpool. My prayers have been answered, I only want to give you the news."

"Brother Stephen." I relented.

"Have you heard, Abbot Huby from Fountains Abbey came and reduced our Abbot to a menial brother and replaced him with someone he brought with him, he will get things sorted out properly."

"No, I hadn't heard, but I am glad, especially for you."

"And I have been talking to some of the pilgrims that have stopped here, their faith and devotion has really impressed me. I can't help thinking how wrong I was to have doubts, how shallow my faith must have been compared to theirs. My faith may have been tested but not to the extremes some of theirs had and their faith shone from them."

"I can see you have changed, you have found peace."

"Yes, I have found peace. So, I don't know if I should be talking to you. I should be devoting my time to prayer."

"You shouldn't really." I said. "But if you get lonely and need a friend there can be no harm in that. But somehow I don't think you will be getting lonely."

Stephen didn't get lonely. There were fairly frequent pilgrims going to or returning from St. David's. He also went into the village more often and got to know the local people. Every Sunday he would hold a service in the chapel and many of the villagers would attend this. So I was content just to rest with nature.

Chapter 27

The Investigation

The earth circled the sun a few times before Stephen wanted to talk to me again. This time he was out of breath having run most of the way from the Abbey. He was too out of breath to actually call my name but there was an urgency that I sensed in his mind.

"Brother Stephen. It is a while, something is wrong."

"I need your help." He managed eventually.

"As long as it isn't a matter of faith again."

"We have a few pilgrims staying at the Abbey so I took extra supplies to them. I found a priest dead in the cloister, I think someone killed him. This has never happened before and none of us know what to do. The Abbot has forbidden anyone to leave but he can only do this for a few days. There is a killer and I don't know if it is one of the pilgrims or one of us."

"What do you expect me to do?"

"I was thinking as I rushed here. You know people, you have so much experience, and you are the wisest person I know."

I smiled at his use of the word person.

He continued. "You could come and stay at the Abbey for a day or two, talk to everyone, you will be able to discover the killer, I am sure you would. But you need to be someone important especially as you are a woman, announce yourself as Lady Moonpool, the Abbot will think you are from an important family and not ask any questions." He paused for a moment, considering. "The only problem, we need to do something about your dress."

A style must have come into his mind because my dress instantly changed, it was now blue and black, silk and lace, and reached to my ankles. He was startled.

"How did you do that?" He asked.

"Actually, you did this, you had a picture in your head. I quite like this, I may keep it." I considered for a moment, then producing a ribbon I tied my hair up. "Now, I am Lady Moonpool."

Stephen nodded. "You are indeed."

Stephen rushed back while I made my own way on foot rather than suddenly appearing there. I wasn't sure that I would be able to enter, but hopefully no iron swords were kept there. As I approached I felt no pain so I carried on. I was able to walk right up to the door and pulled the bell chain.

A startled monk opened the door. I pushed past him, he needed to think I was really important and I had seen how this was accomplished.

"Lady Moonpool, lead me to the Abbot." I said imperiously.

"Certainly Lady Moonpool, come this way." He said, bowing.

He led me round the cloisters to a large oak door. He knocked and waited.

A voice from within said. "Come in."

So he opened the door and led me in.

"Lady Moonpool, Father."

Abbot Cecil turned from looking through the window, he seemed a kindly sort with greying hair, a short and stocky man. He looked rather startled at my presence, women were seldom admitted.

"Abbot Cecil. I am Lady Moonpool and I am on a personal pilgrimage to St David's." I put a foot forward to show I had bare feet. "I am in need of your hospitality for a day or two, my journey has been long."

He took this very calmly. "You are most welcome, we do not have many women visit and do not have suitable accommodation." He thought for a while.

I smiled my most winning smile.

"I know how we can manage, you must use my room as it is farthest from everyone else, I will mingle with the brothers, it will be no hardship and it will be good for my soul."

"You are most generous, Abbot." My kind can be very good at a glamour that humans are very susceptible to, and I have to admit I intentionally exuded a lot of this. Monks are still men after all.

The monk who brought me in was standing open mouthed.

"Brother James." The Abbot said to him. "Go and prepare a cell for me next to yours will you."

And off he went.

"We are about to have our meal and you are welcome to join us. Then we will have vespers where you are also welcome. Would you come with me?"

Abbot Cecil took me to the refectory and had me sit next to him on the end table after moving everyone along. There were five and five and five and five monks and five and five and five and five and five and three lay people, yet all were silent and they stared at me. I quickly searched through the surface thoughts of those nearest to me but found no hint of killing in any of them only a great deal of speculation.

The Abbot rose and said a Latin grace, as he sat again cold meats, cheese and bread and wine was brought round. Then everyone began to eat in silence. I contemplated the food set before me for a moment, then pretending to eat I handed it down to five and three mice I had called to the table under me. The wine I left stating I had taken a vow not to touch alcohol.

Following the meal we were led into a side aisle of the Abbey itself for vespers. I took the opportunity of being in a place of worship to see if The Maker Of All Things would speak to me.

'Oh Maker Of All Things, is it alright for me to be here, doing what I am doing? I should have asked before.'

'You have good instincts, Moonpool, use them.'

That was encouraging, and I got the impression he was smiling at my bumbling interference with human matters yet again.

I don't get involved in religious services but in my human form I did find vespers chanted by the monks quite moving and relaxing.

After vespers those of us who were pilgrims were taken to the small, comfortable library to wait for compline while the community had their own tasks.

"Lady Moonpool?" Began one of the monks from Neath Abbey. "I have never heard of a Lord Moonpool or a Moonpool estate."

"I am from a very old family, Brother Peter, we like to keep out of things. I am here as a sort of penance for getting too involved with ordinary people." Which was sort of true.

"And you walked all the way barefoot, how far is it you have walked?"

"I really can't tell you, I have no idea of distances, I have walking barefoot for a very long time, my feet are used to it. But where are you all from? I gather you are all together."

"We are from Sweyneshe." Said one elderly cleric. "I am Canon of Eglwys Gadairian Sioseff Sant, I was here with Father Edward who was looking after me but he met with an accident, so we wait here for another priest to accompany me. Brothers Peter and Tysil are from Neath Abbey and Geraint and Osian are members of our congregation at the Cathedral. But I must say, it is most unusual for a woman to be staying here, your family must have a great deal of influence for a family I have never heard of."

"An accident?"

"Yes, I am afraid he died. There will be a requiem mass for him tomorrow, you are welcome to attend if you are still here."

"Oh, I am so sorry."

I was feeling a pain in my arm, one of the pilgrims was concealing an iron weapon. The Canon and his two congregation were very open people and I had no bad feeling from them. The two monks were closed and I couldn't read them.

Peter kept looking at my feet which I couldn't hide completely under my dress, he must have noticed they were not the feet of someone walking barefoot over a great distance, I couldn't make them look travel worn.

"Your dress looks so fresh and new, it is hard to imagine you have walked far." Said Peter.

"Call me vain, but this is a new dress I had it this morning. I may be on a pilgrimage and be walking barefoot but you must excuse a woman's pride when coming to so important an Abbey.

"They do sell some nice dresses in Caerfyrddin, it seems like a busy town." Said the Canon. "I don't blame you."

Peter looked askance at me. He was a very closed man and I sensed he always put a barrier around his feelings.

I talked for some time with Geraint about Sweyneshe, I did know the spirit from there but he had kept to himself unlike me, I hadn't heard from him for a long time, so I wasn't sure if he had fallen asleep, but without asking direct questions I was unable to find out.

"Brother Tysil." I said. "You are very quiet, is this your first pilgrimage?"

"He has taken a vow of silence." Said Peter.

"Oh, sorry, please forgive me."

Tysil nodded.

The bell rang for compline so we made our way back to the Abbey. Peter purposely came very close to me, he was asking me something but the burning pain in my arm blotted out what he was saying. I stumbled.

"Are you alright?" The Canon asked as he grasped my other arm to steady me.

"Thank you Canon, I will be."

So I had my answer.

After compline we retired to our cells. The reaction I had with Peter meant that he had an iron weapon and it had spilt blood. He probably still had it on him because he had no opportunity to get rid of it, and he didn't want to leave it somewhere in case it was found. The alternative was that he kept it with him in case he needed it again which was concerning, in which case I needed to act swiftly. I do not need to sleep and I made up my mind what I was going to do, but waited. I waited well into the night. Then I made my move.

I appeared in Peter's room. He had a lit candle and was pacing up and down the small confines of his cell. He saw me appear right in front of him. Immediately my arm began to ache again.

"How," He began. "I knew you were not who you said you were but who are you, what are you that you can appear just like that?"

"I am not Lady Moonpool, just Moonpool. I know you killed a man and you have the weapon on you."

He reached for his weapon but no matter how fast he was I was faster for I am the wind. I had his wrist and since I am tree and grass, soil and rock he could not move.

Slowly I unfurled my wings, I was angry enough to double my size but there was just not enough room, but my wings filled the room anyway and that was enough, and with the candle behind me I cast a huge shadow over him.

"I am a servant of The Maker Of All Things. You must tell me why you took a life."

He cowered before me as much as he could with his wrist caught in my hand.

"In the name of the Son of The Make Of All Things I command you, tell me why you took a life."

Against his will he had to tell the truth, I had invoked the Son and his authority compelled him. A little twist of his arm didn't harm.

"When we were coming here I dropped my bag, the priest caught it and saw what was in it." He squirmed but could not get away and he had to continue through gritted teeth. "I had taken certain treasures from my home Abbey." Again he tried to pull free and tried desperately to speak no more. "I was not going to stay in St. David's but planned to sail across the sea to Ireland, sell the treasures and disappear. I could not risk him telling anyone."

With my other hand I picked up his bag which was on the bed.

"Are you going to tell the Abbot or shall I?" I demanded.

I let him go and since, because he had reached for it, I knew where the long dagger was so I reached into his habit and pulled the dagger out, burning my hand badly before dropping it into the bag. He was a coward so I knew I had to tell the Abbot and I had to tell him before Peter could get away.

I appeared in the Abbot's cell and shook him until he woke up. My wings were still unfurled because he needed to see who I was.

"What? Lady Moonpool, but..."

Before he could fully grasp what was happening I dropped the bag on his bed.

"Here is Peter's dagger, he is the killer, and the treasures he stole from Neath Abbey, you need to capture him before he gets away."

My hand burned so bad and the pain was hard to bear I had to let go of my physical self before I could explain any more.

For some reason the pain was gone immediately, unlike when Llewellyn cut me with his sword.

I sat on a bank outside Cyffig and called out to Silverwheel. I always draw such comfort from her when she sits with me as she did now.

"How is your hand now?" She asked holding it and examining it.

"There is no pain, no redness or anything." I looked at my hand with surprise. "After the time with Llewellyn's sword I was expecting it to last for ages. I actually held that dagger even if only for a short time, and I am sure there was still a trace of blood on it."

"With Llewellyn there was a depth of feeling on your part, so much that you were willing to become human for him, and then there was the sense of betrayal. And, of course he drew blood. With this you were solving a killing, nothing more, you were not emotionally involved."

We said nothing for some time, just enjoyed each other's presence.

"Is that a new dress?" She asked suddenly.

"Yes, Stephen imagined it for me, do you like it? I think I will keep it. Do you like it?"

"Oh, dear. What with now being called Moonpool, and now a new dress, I think you are becoming rather vain."

With that she laughed and moved on.

Early the next day Stephen wanted to see me, I was curious so I stood beside him outside the chapel.

"Well done, Moonpool." He said. "You really are amazing."

"So, did they stop Peter before he got away?"

"Stop him? We found him in the Abbey praying his heart out. He was going on about the angel of retribution, he thought he was going to die and he was going to be dragged into the fires of hell. He wouldn't move."

"The angel of retribution." I smiled. "I forget how scary I can be when I try."

"I find that hard to believe."

"What did the Abbot say?"

"The Abbot said to him, 'Angel of retribution? That was Lady Moonpool, she came to me with your bag, I found her quite charming. I wish she had stayed until the morning so we could thank her.' So there has been a lot of speculation about who Lady Moonpool is."

"So, what do people say?"

"That you must be the wife of some high ranking dignitary sent here to find the killer, though they found it difficult to imagine that a woman would be sent to do a man's work. The Canon said he was determined to track down Lord Moonpool. Peter kept raving about wings filling his room which, of course, no one believed."

"And what did the Abbot say about my wings?"

"Did you appear to him with wings then?" He was surprised. "He didn't mention wings. I didn't know you had wings, I thought Peter was imagining them or it was shadows because of the candle he had.

The Abbot did say he would have liked to ask you a few things."

I unfurled my wings. "These wings. Oh yes, I have wings, but not like an angel."

And I left Stephen stunned.

Chapter 28

Silent Watcher

A woman was crying in such desperation I was drawn to her. She was sitting on the bridge, her legs hanging over the side. It was a cold night, overcast, and a bitter wind was blowing up the valley, the river was full because of the recent rain and is swirled and eddied in its rush to go downstream. I could sense she was considering letting go and dropping into the river so she could feel no more pain and heartache. But there was no one who believed in me at this time so I could not appear to her, I could do nothing if she let herself drop. All I could do was reach into her mind with calm and hope.

"Whose there?" She turned but could see no one.

Her crying eased somewhat and she climbed back on to the bridge. She started creeping carefully up and down, looking here and there.

"I know someone is there."

Now she was frightened. A moment ago she was thinking of ending her life, now she was afraid someone was going to take it from her. Try as I might I could not appear. So I asked an owl to fly down and land on the bridge wall, which he did.

"Oh, an owl."

It took a while for her heart to stop beating so fast.

I wanted to know why she was in such a desperate situation but it was hard to get through the pain and sadness in her mind and in her heart.

The owl moved closer to her and watched her intently.

"Oh, owl, you are wise, can I talk to you and do you understand?"

The owl continued to watch her. He blinked a couple of times but otherwise didn't take his eyes off her.

"My husband had a trade route that took him to Caerfyrddin all the time and I did begin to wonder why he took so long, and there was something in his manner when he returned. Then he sent a message to say he had met someone and wasn't coming back. Now my two boys caught some sort of fever, I prayed and prayed to God to save them but they died anyway. How can life be so cruel, and where is God?"

The owl blinked but still watched her.

"You are the only one I can talk to, the only one who hears."

The owl lifted off and flew to a tree further up the road.

"Hoo." He said, and waited.

Anna followed, puzzled.

When she reached the owl he flew on to a bush further along. She followed again.

Slowly, by bush and wall and gate, he led her back to the village. Quite a crowd had gathered and when they saw her, one woman ran to meet her and threw her arms around her.

"Anna, Anna, we were so worried."

Anna started crying again. "What is there for me? I have lost everything, my husband, my boys."

"You have a community that cares for you, and a sister who loves you, you will come and live with us."

Mai took her into her home while the others dispersed, very much relieved. The owl followed, flew into the house and perched on top of the dresser.

"Is he with you?" Asked Mai.

"Yes, he is a friend."

"What were you thinking, going off like that, I was afraid you were going to do something stupid, I couldn't lose you on top of my nephews. You were so distraught I can understand. I am so glad you didn't, and overjoyed that you came back."

"You can thank the owl for that."

Anna sat by the small stove and warmed herself, rocking back and forward, hunched up. Mai brought some milk and some bread and sat down beside her.

"I am surprised at Dilwyn, he seemed such a nice man." Mai held Anna close. "But to lose your two boys, that is too much. Stay with us, somehow we will get through this."

The door opened and Mai's husband, Cled, came in looking dejected.

The two women looked up, Mai particularly was surprised to see him.

"What is it, Cled?" She asked.

"The Abbey is dissolve, for good this time, I will have to find work somewhere else. I don't know what is going to happen to it, I hear it is being given to some important people in England somewhere, they won't be interested in Whitland at all. And I don't know what is to become of our chapel."

He paused and looked properly for the first time.

"More important, how are you Anna?"

"I have asked her to stay with us, she is so distraught."

"By all means, we don't have much but what we have you are welcome to share."

Anna began to cry again, in all her hurt and grief she realised she was not alone.

As night began to draw in the owl looked at me, he was hungry and wanted to go out to hunt. I nodded and said I would watch for the night. So he flew down off the dresser and landed by the door and started to peck at the door.

"What the …!" Cled burst out almost spilling his beer.

"He is Anna's friend, I think he wants to go out."

"Has he been here all the time?"

Mai let him out and he flew off into the night.

Over the next few days the owl and I kept watch over Anna. She often walked down to St Mary's chapel and would stand outside.

"Why did you let my children die, what hope have I, my life is over and I doubt there is a better life beyond. I cannot live and I cannot die." She shouted eventually.

"Hoo." Said the owl. He was sitting on the bank by the entrance to the churchyard, looking into the west.

"What can you see?"

He walked up and down a bit then looked back into the west. "Hoo."

She stared into the west but saw nothing, only the trees and the hills and the clouds scudding in the blue sky beyond.

Cled came into the house and sat down, tired.

"How is the job in the bakery going?" Asked Mai.

"It is hot work, but it is a good job." He glanced up at the owl. "He is still here then. Have you given him a name yet?"

"He hasn't said what it is." Said Anna. "He keeps wanting me to look at something down by the chapel, up the valley from there. You don't know anything there do you?"

"Only the next village but that is some distance away." Then Cled was thoughtful for a while then he cleared his throat. "I have been asking around, your husband is living openly with this woman in Caerfyrddin, he doesn't care. I have also made inquiries about divorce or annulment, you won't get anywhere with the church unless you have money, which we haven't." He paused a while, the colour rising in his face. "You know people in this village wouldn't blame you if you had another man, as far as they are concerned you are as good as divorced or widowed anyway, and the priest who only comes once a month is not interested in the local people anyway."

"You are a good man, Cled." Said Anna. "Mai is very lucky."

"And another thing." Said Mai. "I don't know if this is the best time to tell you both but I will have to sometime."

"What is it Mai?" Cled asked.

She looked down at her hands which she was wringing. "I am pregnant."

Cled jumped from his chair and hugged his wife, then he reached out and brought Anna into the embrace. Anna's emotions were so confused, happy and desolate at the same time.

I was drawn again to the river where a young man was gazing down into the swirling waters. He was a very open man and without even trying to read his thoughts Anna was very much on his mind.

"There you are you young shirker." Said the loud voice of the blacksmith. "Tools don't deliver themselves, and after that I need you to help fire up the forge."

The young man jumped. "Sorry Gruffydd. I am on my way."

Gruffydd smiled. "Are you going to tell me who she is?"

"I can't. It is impossible."

"Impossible, but you can't stop thinking about her, why is it impossible then? Are you too shy or something?"

"Oh, no. She is married."

"Ah, then you will just have to work twice as hard to put her out of your mind. You are young yet, this will pass." Gruffydd thought for a moment. "It wouldn't be Anna would it?"

The young man sighed.

"Married? She is as good as widowed. Her husband ran off never to come back, he wouldn't dare face the people here. It is not impossible, just rather unusual."

"What do you mean, unusual."

"Just this. This would not be the first time, most people here would be quite happy to accept you and Anna getting together. Because she lost her two boys as well people would be glad to see her with someone, and everyone likes you. There will be the odd person, the occasional whisper and black look but that will pass with time."

Anna often walked about the village and talked to people, they were so understanding and always genuinely pleased to see her. The owl always followed her and he was a source of great interest. She always seemed to bumping into a young man called Idris in different places, she wondered what his job might be for him to seemingly be everywhere.

"Hello owl." He said. "Anna hasn't given you a name yet?"

"Hoo." Said Anna. "That is the only thing he says so it must be his name."

"Hoo." Said the owl.

"Are you going down to the chapel again today Anna?" Asked Idris.

"I thought I might, it is peaceful and I can think."

"Then I will walk with you, that is if you don't mind, I have a little time."

So, silently they walked together down to the chapel. There Hoo sat on the bank and gazed towards the west.

"What is your job, Idris? Surely they will miss you."

"I am apprentice to the blacksmith, mostly I fetch and carry, I bring tools to be mended and take them back when they are done. Gruffydd says I need to get some muscle before I do any really heavy work. But he has started me pumping the forge."

The owl paced up and down then gazed into the west again.

"What is he looking at?" Said Anna.

"Do you know the stories about this place?"

"No, what stories?"

"Stories about a nature spirit who lives here, who is old as the valley."

"No." She looked around, expecting to see someone, not able to imagine what I looked like.

"You have heard of thin places though?"

"What are they?"

"A thin place is somewhere that the veil between this world and the next is very thin, it is a spiritual place. This is why the nature spirit lives here. The owl can probably see into the otherworld and wants you to see something there."

"But I can't."

"That is because you are looking with your eyes and your mind, you need to look with your heart and your soul."

"How do I do that?"

"Open your heart and your soul to the possibility of life beyond, let go of all the negative thoughts you have been hanging on to for so long."

"But it hurts so very much."

"I know." He took her hand. "I know only too well."

He had deep hurts which he had let go of and I could feel Anna reluctantly beginning to let go too. Even though she could not see, hear or feel me I took her other hand.

"Maybe if we ask the nature spirit to help." She said.

"Or maybe if we pray to God."

"I have prayed and prayed to God, he doesn't hear."

"I don't know, I think he sent the owl for some reason."

'Oh, Maker Of All Things, now would be a good time.' I said, reaching out to him. 'The human heart is so fragile.'

'I know.' He replied.

The sun began to sink in the western sky and the veil cleared for a moment.

"I see them." She said as tears welled up again. "I see them and they are happy. Oh, they are gone. But I did see them."

The moment had passed and they still held hands. I looked at the owl and the owl looked at me, time for both of us to go.

Chapter 29

Local Trouble

Two river spirits called me to where their rivers met, they were frightened. Normally we all get on with things without having to consult each other, although we spirits do talk from time to time, but this time it was urgent and they needed me to be there. Colomendy's river flowed into Gronw's at the point where we met. Normally we do not need to be near each other to talk or take on a form that though completely invisible to the humans was nonetheless visible to each other and didn't need a human belief because it was not physical, but these two obviously felt it was important to do so since they wanted to show me something. At first I was startled to see the Abbey had been partially demolished, I had not been keeping an eye on the building when it no longer functioned as an Abbey.

"Look there." Said Gronw, a stocky spirit dressed in blues and greens, his light brown hair flowing down his back.

I looked where he was pointing, on the opposite bank of Nant Colomendy to where we stood some huts had been erected and there was a fire blazing away in the one that was open on one side, and there was the sound of hammering against metal.

"It is an ironworks." Whined Colomendy, a little thin spirit in greys and browns, a shock of black hair on his head.

"So I see." I said. "And rather close to both of you."

"Yes, they need the water." Said Gronw. "And they dip their iron ladles into the rivers to fill their buckets."

"They wash their buckets out in us too, and there are always particles of iron." Moaned Colomendy.

"What are they making here?" I asked. "There is already a forge in Whitland and they make all sorts of iron tools, they till the ground in the valley with iron but it does not affect me. Why are you so concerned about this?"

"Here they are making weapons." Said Gronw. "You surely know about gunpowder and guns. They are making shot for canons."

"Do they have any guns or canons here?"

"No, not yet."

"How are you both? Any pain?"

They both shook their heads.

"I would have expected to." Said Gronw. "Shot for canons are weapons used for killing, but no, neither of us are affected."

"Shot on it's own can do no harm, it is only balls of iron. Let me know if they do bring canons, and let me know how you both are. There is not a lot we can do about this but they need horses to bring the iron here on carts and maybe we can talk to them if necessary."

The shot was regularly transported eastward, and the two spirits remained unaffected, whatever war they were used for was a long way away. There was always a war somewhere, it seems human can't live in peace. My kind have had their battles but because of our agelessness we learned the futility of it. Humans have such short lives they have to learn the same lessons over and over again.

The earth circled the sun many times and then suddenly the land cried out and I felt the ache of it even in spirit form. Canons were passing through the valley towards the west, a steady stream of them that went on most of the day.

Just in time I was aware of a young child rushing across the road to her mother in a panic as it passed through the village. Because of the girls young age, the age when not only was my existence possible but extremely likely, I was able to use her belief to take on human form and lift her out of the way of rushing horses towing a heavy canon. In human form I am still the wind in the trees and was able to move us both to the side where her horrified mother stood screaming. The screaming was replaced by shock and amazement then gratitude as I placed her child into her arms.

"My lady." Said Betrys. "Oh thank you, thank you. How can I ever thank you. I was sure Cerys was going to die."

The proximity to so much iron, especially a weapon of war caused me so much pain that spread from my arm through my body I must have fainted. For the next thing I knew I was lying on a straw bed, Betrys had her arm round my head and trying to get me to drink some beer.

Startled, I sat bolt upright knocking the mug out of Betrys' hand. To be unaware of anything for a time was new experience for me and it was not good.

"How long have I been unconscious?" I asked shaking from head to foot.

"Quite some time, my lady, all the time the canons went through."

I found this quite frightening, I have never slept and certainly never been unconscious in all my long existence. For a moment I didn't know what to think.

"I am sorry, I spilled the beer, I will get more for you, my lady."

"I am not a lady Betrys, I am simply Moonpool. And I am the one who should be sorry."

Of course I still had the beautiful dress that Stephen imagined.

"Moonpool?" Betrys sat back on her chair and contemplated for a moment. "Moonpool, there is something I can't quite remember. Ah, well. I can't thank you enough for saving Carys, though how you were so fast I can't imagine." She held up one of my feet. "But you lost your shoes and I can't find them, probably crushed under the horses hooves or canon wheels. I may have a spare pair somewhere, but they won't be your size, your feet are quite small."

"I don't wear shoes, I need to feel the ground."

"You need to feel the ground? Moonpool, now what would that be in Cymraeg?"

"Pwll'euad."

"Pwll'euad, of course, you are a legend." She paused then awe spread over her face. "Well obviously not a legend because here you are in my house, sitting in my chair, you are a goddess."

"I am not a goddess, I am a servant of The Maker Of All Things sent to watch over the valley."

"Can you do nothing about these soldiers with their canons? And how come you fainted?"

"I cannot interfere and iron has a bad effect on me."

"Can you stay a while, I would feel so much safer especially with Carys running about."

"I can stay."

Carys came and sat on my lap.

"You should have flowers in your hair." Carys stated.

And with that her imagination put flowers in my hair. She stared, open mouthed.

"Oh." She said reaching up to touch the flowers. "That is magic."

"It is your magic that did this, little girls always have magic." I said. "May I keep them?"

"Oh, yes. What else can I magic for you?"

"These flowers are magic enough thank you Carys."

Betrys started peeling vegetables and Carys jumped down and started to play with a rather worn little doll made of rags.

"What are those you are peeling?" I asked Betrys.

"Potatoes."

"Potatoes, they are new aren't they?"

"They have been around for ages, I grew these myself."

"Let me help with those." I said to Betrys.

"Oh, no, that would not be fitting."

I drew my chair over to her and picked up another knife.

"Why can't we all live in peace?" Asked Betrys. "It makes no difference to us if there is a king or some other ruler, if only we could simply get on with our lives."

"It has always been so." I said as I helped her peeling potatoes.

"And you can do nothing?"

"No one listens to us any more, and even when they did they still fought. In time Cromwell will be forgotten and life will still go on because of people like you. You know what I wish, one day someone will listen to me and record my memories on a parchment so hopefully people will learn the futility of politics and power and greed and war, so I can tell of all the people like you who are the heart and soul of humanity."

"Do you think that will happen?"

"No, people will not listen, they will always fight."

"You must get frustrated with people."

"Actually I don't, because there are always far more people like you, like the people of this village. I don't bother with those who think they are important, only those, like you, who are the really important people."

We finished the potatoes.

"Dai will be home soon, will you not stay for the night?"

"Thank you but I need to be by myself. You are a good friend and I am glad to be with you, but I made a choice a long time ago. I may be back tomorrow."

For many days shot was being forged in the ironworks and carts were taking it down to Pembroke. When the air was still we could just make out the distant sound of canons like thunder a long way off. I thought of the people caught up in the siege and the effect it was having on my cousin. Colomendy and Gronw though unaffected themselves felt so helpless, they could do nothing about the production of shot and they, too, thought of our cousins and of the people who were being killed by the shot that was made there.

I continued to visit Betrys for a while, but when the siege ended I came less often so they could get on with their lives. I particularly didn't want to interfere with Carys as she grew, she had to be free to make her own way in life. I settled into the valley, back into nature. The pace of change was too fast with the humans for me but nature, the cycle of the seasons, the circling of the earth round the sun and the dance of the stars was constant. I kept an interest in Carys and gladly watcher her grow, and marry, and have children. I hope she forgot me, but somehow I don't think she did.

Chapter 30

Cyffig School

Cai Jones had dreams. He was the youngest of three boys by many years. His brothers were already working on the farm so he was being sent to Cyffig Church where the Curate had a small school in the tower. He was ambling along the lane this particular morning, the sun rising in the west into a perfect blue sky, the birds singing in the trees as he passed, a squirrel scurried across his path, daffodils lined his way.

"If only someone could tell me about the trees and the flowers and the birds and the animals and the sun and the stars. Mr Phillips is so dull and talks about the bible and the church and maths and reading and writing."

I was drawn to him because his mind was open and he wanted to know so much.

"Please God, send me someone who knows about interesting things."

Nudge.

Rather than appear beside him I appeared some distance behind and called to him.

"Cai, wait for me."

He turned. "Hello, my lady." And he waited for me to catch up.

"I am not a lady, I am just Moonpool. I was walking along and saw you in the distance and I thought I would like to walk with you for a while. Is that alright?"

"Yes, I suppose. You're very pretty."

"Thank you. Where are you going?"

"Mr Phillips has a school in the church tower, but it is very dull, he is boring and the room is dark and smelly. Do you know anything about trees and birds and animals and such?"

So I started pointing out the different trees and how to recognise them, I pointed out the birds that we could see and about their lives, I showed him the signs of where the animals had been and where they lived. Cai soaked it all up, he asked questions and from his questions I realised he was a very intelligent boy. Then we arrived at the church.

"And here we are. Off to school then Cai. Perhaps we will meet again." Then with a backward wave I walked on.

The next day I waited for him at the gate to the farm. It was a bright early morning and there was a cold edge to the light wind.

"Hello miss." He called as he saw me waiting. "I enjoyed out talk yesterday, I am glad to see you again."

"Hello Cai. What did you learn in school yesterday?"

"I learned about Jonah and the whale and I can read quite well now."

We began to walk together.

"What do you know about the sun and the moon and the stars?" I asked.

"Only that by watching where they are my father knows when to sow and when to harvest."

So I told him about the tilt of the earth and the reason for the seasons, I told him about the moon and the tides of the sea and why there were the phases of the moon, I told him about the planets that circle the sun, I told him about the stars and how people told stories about the shapes they saw in them. I saw wonder in his eyes as we talked, he wanted to know everything.

Then we reached the church again.

"Won't you come in and meet Mr Phillips and perhaps he will let you tell the others some of these things."

"No, Cai, Mr Phillips is a Curate, I might confuse him."

"Why?"

"Off you go."

I waited for him by the gate again. It had rained in the night and the ground was wet and puddles had formed in patches.

"Oh, miss." He said. "You don't have any shoes."

"I need to feel the ground. Did you learn anything interesting yesterday at school?"

"I leaned that Jesus fed five thousand men with a few loaves and fishes, it was a miracle you know. It would be useful to have him around now."

"He is, it is just you can't see him."

"I wish he would give my Mam some extra bread, she is always grumbling me and my brothers eat too much."

Off we went again.

"And we did sums, I am not very good at sums." He went on.

"I can't help you there I am very bad with numbers, but you have to try hard."

I talk to him about the herbs and their healing abilities and where to find them, and before we knew it we arrived at the church.

Mr Phillips was waiting by the gate. He wasn't impatient, just curious.

"Jones, why are you always late?"

"I was talking with this lady."

"Lady. Too much imagination you have. Now in you come and hurry."

Cai turned and waved and I waved back, then he hurried into the church.

The next day Cai was very thoughtful.

"I tried to tell Mr Phillips about you but he told me not to be so silly, he said I was too clever for fantasies. But he saw you, he must have."

"No, perhaps not. Mr Phillips as a very learned and practical man, a man of strict beliefs."

"How could he not see you?"

"You need to believe to see me and his particular beliefs wouldn't allow him to see me, I am not really a person like you I am a nature spirit."

"What is a nature spirit?"

"The Maker Of All Things made everything that you see, and he made angels to look after the important things like worlds and countries and people, and he made us to look after nature. He put me in this valley to be guardian of the valley and to try and infuse peace into the people who live here, it doesn't always work, and I do try to look after as many people as I can but I can't watch everyone there are too many people, but sometimes I interfere a little too much."

We were both quiet for the rest of the journey, he was deep in thought, trying to work out what this meant. Mr Phillips was waiting for Cai again.

"Ignore me." I said. "He doesn't see me so you had better not either, now go, we will speak again tomorrow."

The following morning I waited for him again. When he came to the gate he saw me and bowed.

"What is that for?" I asked.

"I asked my mother about nature spirits. She said there are legends, old legends about a goddess in the valley, but we don't believe in such things now. You are a goddess then."

We started to walk.

"I am not a goddess, I am a servant of The Maker Of All Things. I think he has allowed me to talk to you because my time surely should be over now. But maybe he has some great plan for you. People are doing all sorts of things now. They are sailing round the world and discovering new countries. They can make their own lightning. They can make things with glass that help them to look out into the stars. They can heat water to make steam to work machines. I think The Maker Of All Things wants you to think beyond what Mr. Phillips can teach you, he wants you to look deeply into things and think for yourself."

"Oh, I hope your time isn't over."

"If it is then I am content. But I am enjoying talking to you while I can."

"When I grow up I want to talk to you still."

"When you grow up I know you will leave the valley, I have heard Mr Phillips talk to your parents, he wants you to go away to study when you are old enough and to perhaps be a scientist or engineer. And if I have in my small way opened your mind to greater possibilities that is enough for me."

"Even if I am a scientist I will come back some day to talk to you again."

"Don't promise, it would be nice to know how you get on but you have your life ahead of you."

As the seasons passed I told him as much as I could about the natural world, I told him as much as I could about history but from my perspective, and I told him much of my story. Many times as we walked he would be carrying a book back to Mr Phillips which he had given him to read.

Eventually, when he was old enough, he did move away to study, I did hope he might write about me but he didn't. On one occasion, when he was quite grown, he was visiting his family and he called for me at the gate. We walked to the church and he talked about things I didn't really understand, he was a chemist and was grateful for some of the things I had told him, but he had gone way beyond my understanding of nature. At the church he took my hand and kissed it.

"Goodbye Moonpool and thank you for everything."

Chapter 31

Iron Road

Men were digging, digging in the depths of the earth, by the light of lamps with hammer and chisel, pick and shovel. I became aware of them when they passed the point where the land I am guardian began in the west. I then became aware of more men peering through tubes on tripods at others with tall sticks with lines all down one side, they were slowly marking out a route through the valley, passing between St Mary's and Whitland on and on towards the east. And all the time the men were digging in the depths.

There was no one who now believed in my existence so I couldn't ask anyone what was happening, I just had to watch and wait.

What made this so hard for me was that the digging men were tunnelling through a hill that had once been on one side of Little Rainbow's waterfall, I felt somehow this was a desecration of her memory. There were a family up in Llanddewi Velfrey who had her blood in them which still ran quite strong but they knew nothing of their heritage and whatever was going on was nowhere near them. If anyone was to still see me it would be them, I wondered what influence I could exert on them.

The men kept digging, digging, soon there would be a tunnel right through the hill but what for I couldn't imagine.

I asked Silverwheel, she would know because she can see the whole world.

"Silverwheel, why are these men digging a tunnel, why are they marking a line across the valley?"

"You know about a machine powered by steam. When they lay an iron road they can move this machine along it and it pulls carriages with people or produce in behind it. They are doing it in many parts of the world, they have built this iron road as far as Caerfyrddin already. People can go from place to place without horses because of the steam engine, but only where the iron road is. And they can move many things about as well rather than in carts."

"Is it dangerous? Does the iron road affect us?"

"You know humans, there is always danger somewhere. Mostly we are not affected by it, well I should say you and the other spirits on the earth, they are not going to get to the moon."

"Then I don't need to worry."

"No. It does mean that there will be a lot more coming and going of people, and for you it will mean that the village of Whitland will grow because from their perspective it brings trade and money if they build a stopping place for the train."

"I can't keep up with all the people there now, I can't keep up with the changes that happen so fast. For all we know they will be able to get to the moon."

Quite unexpectedly Sofiel asked me to St. Mary's. By the Angel's authority I was able to take on human form.

We appeared together on a new road that cut through the edge of the old enclosure and went over a new stone bridge. The church had gone and there were men digging, digging in the ground.

"What is this?" I asked.

"Because of the new railway coming through Whitland a new church is being built, looking at the area they are digging it is going to quite a big one." Said Sofiel.

"That is a good thing, isn't it."

"Oh, yes, but you and I haven't seen so much change in so short a time have we. Oh, and I see you have a new dress."

"Yes, Stephen imagined it for me to investigate a murder."

"I know all about that, you did well, Moonpool. It is such a pity that the Abbey has gone, but at least these humans intend for our church to continue."

I took the opportunity to look about me. Whitland had grown and was now almost to the church, and from here I could see digging where the iron road would be laid.

"Such changes, I don't know if I can keep up." I said. "Could you call me back when the church is finished, I would like to have a look at it."

Suddenly I felt a pull to the tunnel that was being built. One of the men was placing a silver coin into a crack in the stone.

"What is that for Will?"

"You can't be too careful in this job." Said Will. "The gods need to be appeased when you are digging in their land like this."

"You did that last week." Said another man.

"Different god. Didn't you feel it the other day? That one felt like a crow or something, darker than this one. This one feels quite bright and friendly, but even so these gods need some offering."

"You and your gods."

All the men laughed.

"We don't want to anger them and have the roof fall in." Insisted Will. "We all know this is a dangerous job."

"Enough chat." Came a shout from the end of the tunnel. "We have a tunnel to dig."

"We?" Muttered one of the men. "He means us, I can't see him touching a shovel."

The men picked up their tools and started chipping away at the rock. In that enclosed space the noise would have been deafening.

I found Will interesting. As he hammered away with his hammer and chisel he muttered quietly to himself asking an unknown spirit for protection and with every hammer blow he apologised. I watched for a while, fascinated. This was slow work but it was steady and rhythmical and gradually the work progressed.

But then Will's chisel hit a fissure and suddenly the wall of rock in front of him began to move.

Using his simple belief in the gods I took on human form and because of the danger I appeared twice my usual size. I put my back against the wall.

"Stand back, Will, and all of you." I commanded.

Whether it was because of my command or the shock of seeing this large form appear before them at least they moved back. Slowly I eased away from the wall and a large rock slid from the wall and some smaller rocks and a lot of dust fell from the ceiling. I let them settle then I shrank back to my normal size. Because I too am rock I was unharmed by this but I was covered with dust.

"It should be safe now." I said. "I would get someone to check it first though before you carry on."

All the men were on their knees now.

"My lady." Said Will. "I apologise, I didn't expect a goddess, I hope we have not desecrated your land with all this tunnelling. But no, you just save our lives, how can we thank you."

"You already did, Will, you put a coin in the wall." And I was gone, and with that the dust that had covered me fell to the ground.

The other men didn't laugh at Will now, in fact they all put coins in cracks in the walls.

Slowly, slowly the men dug away at the tunnel. Men dug along the route marked out for the iron road and stones were tipped in. The season passed and Sofiel called to me again.

Sofiel can appear very human at need and chose to appear as a man in a smart suit and a bowler hat, even though angels don't have a gender. By Sofiel's authority I was able to appear.

"That dress is very suitable for the occasion, Moonpool. It is good that Stephen changed it for you, Ban's dress would have been too short for a public event like this."

We were at the front of a large crowd, those nearest to us were rather surprised by our sudden appearance but, as often happens with grown humans, shook their heads and thought they just hadn't seen us arrive.

We managed to be standing at the open gate in the new wall that cut across the edge of the enclosure.

"Ladies and gentlemen. Welcome to your new church." Shouted a very dignified man to much applause.

He stood with a group of men including a Bishop.

The new church was very large and beautiful. The high stone wall facing us was topped by a single bell in a bellcote that leaned slightly inwards, large windows were set in the wall that would allow the setting sun to shine in.

"This is a church that St. Mary herself would be proud to be patron of. I have employed the best architect from France and the best stonemasons from Swansea. Glaziers from Bristol and carpenters from Bath. So I know you will be proud to call this your church. We even have our own Vicar separate from Llanboidy, the Reverend Evan Rowland who later today is to be inducted by Bishop Connop Thirlwall this evening, you are all welcome to attend. But first, I wish to show you your new church."

More applause.

"Do come in and marvel at the interior."

We entered the gate to the path. Sofiel and I were greeted by warm handshakes, Angels are always very attractive when they appear in human form and my kind do have this glamour about us.

"I am so glad to see so important visitors, I haven't seen you about the village."

"Lord and Lady Moonpool at your service Mr. Yelverton." Said Sofiel.

"You are most welcome, have you come far?"

"In a way we have."

Mr. Yelverton bowed and ushered us in through the stone and wood porch. Inside I was surprised at the light and space of the church. It had a very steep pitch on the roof making it very high inside, there was a very colourful stained glass window over the altar while all the other windows were filled with delicate pastel shades that made the place very light.

"You like it very much don't you Sofiel." I said.

"Yes, very much indeed, I will be glad to have a presence here."

"I can tell because you are glowing."

Angels do tend to glow and Sofiel couldn't help but glow now. So we decided to let go our physical appearance so as not to draw too much attention.

"Thank you Moonpool for keeping us safe." Said Will putting down his hammer and chisel as the dirt and dust settled and he blinked in the bright sunlight.

They had tunnelled through the hill and incredibly they had come out exactly in line with the track ready for the iron road. He so wanted to see me that I appeared beside him.

So shocked and surprised were Will and the other men that they all got down onto their knees.

"Get up, all of you. I am glad to see you all this side of the tunnel safe."

Slowly they did all stand up, but kept their heads bowed.

"My lady." Said Will taking his cap off and looking down at his hands. "We owe you our lives. I never expected a goddess, and one so beautiful."

"Can you tell me about this iron road and what it is for?"

"Railways are being built all over the country to make it easier and faster to travel, our new steam engines can pull many coaches and wagons, this is an exciting new time. This line is going all the way to the coast, from there you can catch a ferry to Ireland."

"Human are so impatient, they want to be somewhere else the moment they start, they are never satisfied." I sighed. "I miss so much that has gone for ever, now change is happening so fast I am not sure I want to be around any more. Thank you Will for believing so I can see the world for the last time, yet I am sad to have seen such times and now I will go to sleep and be forgotten at last."

"Oh, don't say that, my lady, this will always be your valley and you will always be needed."

I looked at him for a while, then holding him under his chin lifted his head to face me. I kissed him on the forehead and then I was gone.

Chapter 32

Seeking Fairies

I found myself drawn to and area on the bank of the Marlais, across the fields from the Vicarage. Two girls were kneeling, seemingly in fervent prayer, but it was a wish they were saying together.

"Oh, please fairies, show yourselves to us, we know you are there, we believe in you. We promise we will not tell."

"Now Lottie." Said one of the girls.

With that one of the two threw a small silver coin into the river, she was very much older and I realised they were not related, but Lottie must have been looking after the younger girl.

Their belief was so great I could feel the pull of their plea like a silver cord. Marlais must have felt it too, he had never taken on human form before because he had never been asked but he was much too unsure of how it was done and I could feel the dilemma within him.

"What do I do?" He asked. "What should I do?"

"Hold back for now." I told him. "Let us wait and see."

We both waited. How many times I have waited I cannot count. Fairies after all are the smaller spirits not Marlais and certainly not me. The fairies in this area are rather prone to mischief and I didn't really want them teasing these girls. Yet Marlais and I both felt the pull very strongly, I trust him but he is not used to human feelings and feelings could be misread on both sides. If I could talk to him away from this but this may be his only chance. If I help him appear I must appear too.

'Oh Maker Of All Things, do we appear, will it harm?' I waited for a while then answered my own question. 'You are right, we should not appear, we should not interfere.'

'Why not? If you do not the fairies will and they will cause more harm.'

Marlais was a thin spirit dressed in browns and greens, with light brown hair that cascaded down his back and beard that flowed upon his chest.

The younger girl screamed and Lottie gathered her into her arms.

"There, Mary, be careful what you wish for, these must be the fairies you wanted to see."

"But they are so big, fairies are small." She cried.

"Fairies are small." I said. "We are not fairies, Marlais is the spirit of the river and I am spirit of the whole valley."

Mary turned her attention to me and stopped crying.

"You are so pretty, you must be a fairy."

If Mary had not been so young I would have been insulted by being called a fairy. Perhaps I am a little touchy about it but fairies are the spirits of flower and leaf and never consider the consequences of their actions.

"I am guardian of the whole valley from here to Llanboidy, and my name is Moonpool."

Lottie slowly released her grip. She looked at the two of us with stunned silence. She was too old in the modern era to believe in us, it was Mary's belief that we were able to appear. Yet Lottie having Irish parents still had enough belief to see us as Mary did.

"Moonpool." Said Lottie after studying me for a while. "That is a pretty name, but where is the pool?"

"Once this whole valley was a lake. I got my name from the moon's reflection in the lake. But that was a long time ago."

"How long ago? You cannot be much older than I am."

"I am older than the world, I just don't age."

Mary reached out her hand towards me and I took hold of it.

"You feel real." She said.

"I am and I am not. I am a real spirit and I can take on human form, but this is not my natural state."

"What are you really?" Asked Lottie.

"I was put here by The Maker Of All Things to be a guardian of the valley."

"And you are not an angel."

"No, angels are more spirit than I am, I am spirit but I am also of the earth." I sat down on the ground and Mary came and sat on my lap

"Then, Mary, we had better not tell your grandfather about them, he really would not approve." Warned Lottie.

"Why not?" Asked Marlais.

"He's the Vicar and he has been going on and on about people fascinated with fairies these days, saying that they are pagan and have nothing to do with Christianity, he doesn't quite go as far as saying they are demonic."

"Pagan, I suppose I am, but I know the Son of The Maker Of All Things quite well." I smiled. "But why are people so fascinated with fairies now?"

"It is this modern world, ever since the coming of the railways many people have been wishing for a simpler life, for simpler, slower times. They see the fairies as being closer to nature, away from all these new-fangled things."

"Fairies, nature spirits, yes we are all closer to nature. Also I must admit I cannot get used to the speed of change."

In all this time Marlais was looking about him, at his river, at the hills, at the trees, at the birds, he stared at Lottie for some time, then smiled down at Mary. Mary looked up at him and smiled.

"Your nice too." She said to him. "But where are the fairies?"

"Oh, be careful of the fairies, they aren't as sweet and innocent as they look. They can be rather naughty." He laughed.

"And be careful of Marlais, he is spirit of the river and rivers can be dangerous." I said and winked at Mary.

"What about you? Are you dangerous?" Lottie asked me.

"I can be. I could tell you some stories."

"Will you?" Asked Mary.

I began to feel that our time was over here.

"I had better not. The Maker Of All Things gave us permission to come but now I think he wants us to go.

Goodbye Mary, I hope you forget about us as you grow up, and do not tell your grandfather about us, it isn't a secret but he will be cross. Lottie, you are already grown up but try and put us out of your mind." It was warm and the air was quite still and heavy, bees were buzzing lazily about the clover and crickets chirped in the long grass, Marlais' river gurgled softly, I could induce drowsiness over them. "Perhaps you both fell asleep here and this is only a dream." They fell asleep and we were gone.

Chapter 33

Three Sisters

It was a day early in the year and the winter was not yet at its deepest though the shortest day had passed. There was no snow but the sky was grey and a cold wind blew from the east. A funeral was taking place in the Church and the coffin, followed by the family and the mourners had come out and processed to the grave.

It was not the sadness of the occasion that caught my attention, although it was of the young husband of a young woman with three small girls in tow and I understood a baby boy back home, I have seen so much sadness among humans. Yet I must admit I really felt the grief that was evident here. The young man had died on Christmas Eve and I know that this would mar all their Christmases. I felt for the three little sisters in their warm coats and black hats.

It was the youngest of the three that so caught my attention. Much smaller than the other two, so young she could not understand what was going on, she only knew a deep, deep sadness and her father was not there to comfort her. Yet I saw in her a spark of joy and laughter that would be her strength through all the sadness and hardness of her life, the spark that appeared now rarely in the descendants of Little Rainbow. Although her blood was mixed with so many people from so many places the Blood of Little Rainbow did indeed flow strongly in this girl's veins. Her great grandmother, Lottie, had married Levi through who the blood of Little Rainbow ran but it was in this little girl that the soul of Little Rainbow was strongest.

If only I could appear to her. I could stand with her but humanity had gone so far from my kind I didn't know if she would be the one with the belief for me to appear to after all this time. Her sorrow was too great for me to press her now. I could only stand with her and hope in her childish innocence that she knew I was there.

The earth turned again and many days passed. Again the same family were there and this time the small coffin held their little brother. I so wanted to hold the little girl but I could not. The grief of the family was intense as it always is when a child dies. Their mother's heart was close to breaking and she held on to her husband's mother because she was a woman of such compassion and love, and being Lottie's daughter had a deep understanding of the spirit in nature and knew in the depths of her being that this was a very thin place, and here they were closest to those they could not see, a woman of unshakeable faith in The Maker Of All Things.

Once more many days later they came again and this time their mother had passed, her heart had broken, grief was too much for her. Even in spirit form I felt deeply the anguish. The little girl lost in a world that at times was hard and lonely. But I saw the love her grandparents had for the three girls and I knew they were safe for Rosanna could almost reach out to me and me to her.

So I watched and I waited, somehow this daughter of Little Rainbow would help me to be remembered. A little girl now who could not fully understand what was happening to her, I knew her life would be hard so I stayed close.

Chapter 34

New Vicar

I stood with the angel in the church, both of us unseen by the people who had gathered. It was not often I came inside but this occasion I felt was important. We watched the ceremony as the new Vicar was inducted.

"I know why you are here." Sofiel said with a smile.

"Do you mind?"

"Not at all. We do not meet enough despite being so close."

"Sorry."

"No it is just as much my fault."

"So, you know why I am here. You know he has met my kind before."

"Yes but he has mostly shut himself down. Rather he has been worn down."

"If only we can open him up again."

"We?"

"I was hoping you could help. You are closer to The Maker Of All Things and know his plans."

"I do not know his plans but I do know this man was brought here for a reason."

We stood unseen in the midst and watched the ceremony continue.

"Did you see the look that passed between him and Little Rainbow's daughter?" Sofiel asked.

"Yes, I did."

"Work on that."

It helped that The Vicarage was opposite Little Rainbow's daughter for it meant they would meet often and their friendship would grow. The spark of joy in her heart would melt the ice in the heart of the Vicar. And so it did, at first it was a good friendship or so it seemed, there was a bond between them that was the basis for a deep and lasting love.

People saw the change in him. As the earth revolved around the sun so his heart and his soul opened up. She believed in him as no one else had and he grew in confidence.

Her love for him and his for her melted his heart and as he began to believe again he remembered an event in his childhood, and event that happened when he was older than when children easily believe in my kind and that was significant. Who the nature spirits were I do not know, nor why they appeared to him.

I cannot say why I was so keen to appear to him, somehow I thought it was important rather than a specific need I had to meet with a human being again although I did anyway. I could not take on human form, the time when people believed in our existence was gone, so I had to rely on planting ideas. Since this Vicar had met my kind before he was perhaps my last chance to take on human form, but he would have to remember his earlier meeting and believe in us again. I did wonder if Silverwheel had any suggestions, she knew the wider world and what possibilities there were.

"He needs to be interested in local history, he needs to find out more about the parish he is Vicar of." She suggested. "After all, if he is to find you it is in the history of the place, and I mean the real history and not what is taught by humans."

"He doesn't seem that interested in history at all."

"In his training he was introduced to a history more relevant to him than lists of kings."

"But how do we get him interested in the history of the valley?"

"There is a course that Lampeter are doing that I am sure he would be interested in."

"He has no interest in studying."

"Little Rainbow's daughter would be interested in him studying. Plant the thought in her mind."

After a trip to Carmarthen to a Church event where Lampeter College was promoting courses for study the Vicar enrolled in a course of Celtic Christianity which led to him researching the ancient history of his parish. Although he wasn't actively looking beyond the Roman occupation I was able to subtly point out to him a much earlier history. So even after he finished the course he continued to look into the earlier history, especially as Bishop Wyn suggested he did.

Before every funeral and every wedding he would stand outside the church, just inside the gate and wait for the hearse or the bride. I suggested that he look around at the shape of the graveyard. He looked round, he walked to the other side of the church and looked, he walked to the back of the church and he looked again. An idea began to develop in his mind. Because of Little Rainbow's daughter's friendship with a local farmer the Vicar became friendly with him, this farmer knew a great deal of the history of the area and told them that there had once been a lake there.

With all the changes that have happened in recent times, motor cars, electricity, even space flight, I cannot keep up. But apparently because of something called the internet you can look down from machines that people have put in orbit around the earth and see the ground from above, and this is what he did. He viewed the graveyard from above and saw the unmistakable elliptical shape of the graveyard and realised that it was an ancient worship site going back to the time when the lake disappeared from the valley and exposed my special place. He worked out the alignment with the rising sun of the equinox. I got quite excited at this, if only he could make the connection with this and his early memories he would have the belief for me to appear to him.

The autumn equinox fell on a Sunday and he had an early service in St Mary's. He came down very early while it was still dark so he could watch the sun rise to make perfectly sure he had the alignment right. As he waited he reflected, he remembered his earlier meeting with nature spirits, he understood the significance of the worship site and he stood at the centre just outside the porch and waited.

The sky was brightening in the east and then suddenly the sun began to peep above the hill and the alignment was obvious. In that instant he knew and in that moment of understanding I felt his belief in me though he didn't know me. I took the opportunity, I reached out to his belief and I took on human form behind him. For a moment I glanced around me at the world that had changed and had remained the same, the familiar contours of the land had not changed, the sounds of the river flowing in its course, the rustle of leaves on the trees, the small sounds of scurrying animals, the early morning song of the birds. The sight of the sun rising over the hill that I had seen so many times as people used to gather to watch, and now this one man was watching.

I could hear the quickening beat of his heart as realisation dawned on him, his slow steady breath. I prepared to speak and hoped I wouldn't startle him too much. I spoke.

"Moonpool."

Chapter 35

Moonpool Revelation

The voice behind me startled me for a moment, I hadn't heard anyone coming and I was deep in thought. It felt strangely as if the realisation that the churchyard was indeed a henge aligned with the rising sun of the equinox had caused the voice and perhaps it was only my imagination. It was the voice of a young woman but had an edge of earthiness as if the valley itself had spoken.

I turned and a woman was standing there, the voice had not been my imagination.

She was average height, long dark almost black hair tied up behind and adorned with blue flowers. Her skin was pale and her eyes were a penetrating blue that seemed to look deep into my soul. She was dressed in a dress of lace and silk that seemed oddly out of place, the sort of dress women of the Victorian age or earlier would wear. She was barefoot.

I could do nothing but repeat the word she had spoken.

"Moonpool."

I could not guess her age, she seemed young, in her early twenties, but there was a wisdom and intensity in her deep eyes that spoke of extreme age. She was smiling slightly and I got the strong impression she could read my thoughts. She was waiting for me to say something and I felt this was a test and it was very important what I said next.

'Hello.' Or 'Good morning' seemed utterly inappropriate. Although I had never seen her before I could not ask if she was visiting because I knew in the depths of my being that I was the newcomer and she had always been here. Yet there was something about her that I did recognise.

There was something about her that I felt rather than knew. Something about her that was of the very land I had glimpsed every time I had come back into the valley and seen the view stretched out below. I could almost feel her thought in mine and her smile widened encouragingly with my train of thought.

"You are ..." Do I take the risk and say what I thought or will it sound stupid if she was simply a young woman who had wandered into the churchyard?

But Moonpool, which was obviously her name, was not a name you would expect anyone to have. I knew from my research there had been a lake here once long ago, and perhaps the name had some relevance to that. Perhaps the lake had reflected the moon to early settlers.

"... a nature spirit." If she laughs then she laughs, I can always say she looked like one.

"You are lucky you didn't say fairy." She said.

I was still not sure. I knew I was not asleep but one does not just meet nature spirits and yet...

"You are the valley."

She nodded. If she was just humouring me we could laugh about it after but I really didn't think she was.

There was something about her that was not human, something otherworldly yet of the very soil.

"You have enough faith in me so I can appear to you, why do you still hold back? You have met my kind before, you know what I am."

"Yes." I said. "But even so, so much of modern thinking has shut itself off from the possibility."

"I know it only too well." She sighed. "You are the first person for such a long time that is willing even to accept the possibility of my existence, and more than that in this moment you actually believe I am here or else I couldn't be."

"I have so many questions."

"No, you have so many answers. You have already worked it out for yourself slowly and steadily. You know where I am in the order of spiritual beings, you had to do that as a follower of the Son of The Maker Of All Things and the experience you had with my kind before. Trust you feelings now and I can show you more and then you will have no doubts."

With that huge, dark, butterfly wings spread upon her back and she smiled at my astonishment

I stepped back in amazement. A sort of wonder and awe. In my last encounter it was only the smaller nature spirits who had wings.

"Why have you appeared to me?"

"Because you believe and because I would ask a favour."

"I would like to help if I can. I have always felt that I missed something important last time I encountered your kind."

"You are one of the very few who now truly believe, we have lost touch and humanity tramples on nature and no longer trusts us. Tell them about me so that people will believe in us again and bring some magic back into the world. Humanity needs us more than ever before, we can heal the world if you let us."

"I will willingly tell them but no one will take me seriously."

"I realise that. You will have to put it in such a way that people will not be sure about the truth of what you say and we will have to leave them to decide for themselves. I will give you certain facts that you can weave into a story and if you can get people to listen to the story we can only hope for the best."

She turned to look behind her.

"You are not expecting anyone yet are you?" She asked.

"I came down early just to watch the sun rise and make sure of the alignment of this place, it will be at least an hour before anyone comes for the service."

"An hour? I still don't know how much time that is. Is it long?"

"Not really. It depends what facts you want me to weave into a story and how far back these facts go."

"Back to the first human who came here, when there was a lake."

"Just after the last ice age."

"Yes."

"Then an hour is not nearly long enough."

"But long enough for you to realise you are not dreaming?" She smiled. "Shall we sit in the porch?"

She folded her wings away, then went into the porch and sat on the side, I followed and sat facing her. I was not dreaming yet it all seemed so unreal, I was excited and rather awe struck to think this woman was a nature spirit, she was the very embodiment of the valley I now called home.

"An hour may not be long enough but we can meet from time to time and I can tell you something each time."

"You are a spirit, does that mean you are older than the Earth or were you created with it?" I asked. There were so many questions I had to start somewhere.

She looked beyond me, beyond the wall of the porch, beyond the valley. "I had witnessed the Maker Of All Things bring the cosmic forces and matter together in this corner of the galaxy, I has seen the small star that was to provide light here being formed and the smaller bodies that surrounded it. I was brought down onto this one and saw that which was to be the moon smashed off from it, I saw the rocks cool, the waters spread, and growing things appear on the land. I saw life begin and the creatures that roamed about develop and die and develop again. I was here as the ice came and went many times over the land I was given to protect and I watched as a valley was carved and filled with a lake, a place of beauty and peace."

Then she fixed me with a penetrating gaze. "But my perceptions changed when the first human came to my lake and just stood. I had heard of them but until then I had not seen one. This creature didn't drink but just stood gazing. I could not understand why it just stood there, was it waiting for something or was something going on in its inner being? But I realised I was waiting too, and this surprised me because I had no perception of time until that moment."

Milton Keynes UK
Ingram Content Group UK Ltd.
UKHW012317011223
433582UK00004B/38